CHANCE OF LOVE

CHANCE OF LOVE

SCANDAL MEETS LOVE 6

DAWN BROWER

MONARCHAL GLENN PRESS

Chance of Love Copyright © 2019 by Dawn Brower

All rights reserved.

Cover art by Mandy Koehler

No part of this book may be reproduced in any form or by any electronic or mechanical means, including information storage and retrieval systems, without written permission from the author, except for the use of brief quotations in a book review.

Trust your heart if the seas catch fire, live by love though the stars walk backward.

— E.E. CUMMINGS, *DIVE FOR DREAMS*

CONTENTS

Prologue	1
Chapter 1	13
Chapter 2	24
Chapter 3	35
Chapter 4	46
Chapter 5	57
Chapter 6	68
Chapter 7	79
Chapter 8	91
Epilogue	102
Afterword	107
About The Author	109
Also by Dawn Brower	111

EXCERPT: LOVE ONLY ME

Chapter 1	119
Chapter 2	130

DAWN BROWER	*Excerpt: When an Earl Turns Wicked*	
	Prologue	145
	Chapter 1	161

DAWN BROWER	*Excerpt: Confessions of a Hellion*	
	Prologue	175

PROLOGUE

April 1816

Spring had always been her favorite season. Lady Lenora St. Martin didn't have much else to look forward to and the very idea of new beginnings appealed to her. Every spring new life sprouted and the barren landscape was filled with beauty and wonder. That also applied to the London ballrooms. New debutantes were launched in society and the latest crop of true English beauties was put on display for those gentlemen in search of a wife.

Lenora had never been considered a beauty…

She'd accepted her lot in life a long time ago. She had dark brown hair and hazel eyes, both boring. Her attributes along with her shyness kept her position as a wallflower secure. No one noticed her and most of the time that was all right with her. A crowded ballroom tended to bring out her worst anxieties. Her cousin Bennett, the Marquess of Holton, insisted she attend social gatherings. Lenora understood his reasons even if she didn't particularly agree with them. Bennett hoped she'd find a suitor, fall in love, and then marry so she could have a family of her own. All of those things sounded wonderful. None of them were likely to happen. At least not with her…

This ball, the one most debutantes and their mothers clamored to attend, was a good example. The young misses were all flirting with their gentlemen suitors and their mothers gossiped with other matrons. The wallflowers did what they did best—hugged the walls. Lenora; on the other hand, did none of that. She didn't merely stand by the wall hoping some wayward gentleman would discover her and lead her to the dance floor. That would have been too simple and probably preferred by her cousin. No, Lenora didn't do anything by normal standards. She hated to be noticed and would have loved to have remained at home reading one of her favorite novels. So she attempted to make the best of a terrible situation and hid in the darkest most obscure corner she could find.

Spring might mean new beginnings, but it also meant new social gatherings. It led to her greatest discomfort and she dreaded it. If she'd been left alone to walk in the gardens or bask in the warmth of sunlight streaming through her bedroom window she'd have been gloriously happy. Instead she was forced into ballrooms and hiding in corners.

"What's a lovely woman such as yourself doing in this dark corner?" His voice was as warm as honey on a hot summer day. It's tempting sweetness washed over her and made her crave a taste…of something. He was also the biggest rake in all of London. Julian Everleigh, the Duke of Ashley was a notorious seducer. "Come dance with me little mouse."

Lenora wrinkled her nose at his endearment for her. She adored Julian, but she knew better than to accept anything he offered. He visited her cousin often enough she should be unaffected by his flirtations. They thrilled her though and she wanted to savor them whenever he deigned to speak to her. "No thank you," she said softly. "I'm all right, promise."

He chuckled lightly and then tilted his lips

upward into the most sinful smile she'd ever witnessed. Not that she'd seen many… Most gentlemen failed to notice her let alone smile purposely in her direction. "You shouldn't promise something that isn't true little one," he said. "I don't ever bother with a promise because I know myself too well. I'll break them the first chance presented to me." Julian winked at her and it sent flutters through her stomach she'd never felt before in her entire life. "Instead I'll ensure you will never forget dancing with me. I'm quite good at it." He held out his hand. "Now please, do me the honor of spending a few moments with me. I'm in desperate need of protection from unwanted advances." He leaned down just enough so that she could feel his warm breath when he spoke. "Are you willing to be my savior?"

In that moment she'd have promised him anything, but she held back. He said promises were nothing to him. The duke openly admitted to breaking them often. The vow she was about to make would be empty words to him. So instead she smiled, even if it was a little wobbly. Dancing in front of everyone terrified her. "I can try…"

"That's all anyone can ask," he told her.

Why did he have to be so gorgeous? He was too

handsome and way too pretty to be paying any attention to her. His golden blond hair rivaled the sun in brilliance and his blue eyes were more dazzling than the most exquisite sapphire. She could easily become lost in his charming veneer if she allowed herself to be. "I supp…suppose," she stuttered over the word. Lenora cleared her throat and began again. "I suppose that is true."

"So?" He lifted a brow. "Will you join me for the next set?"

She nodded as the strands of a waltz filled the room. Lenora almost groaned when she realized what she'd agreed to. The waltz was the most intimate dances and she'd never danced one with a male other than her cousin. Heck, she'd never danced at all with a male besides her cousin… That didn't detract from her dilemma. A waltz with the duke would cause a stir and she'd be so close to him… Her hand shook as she placed it in his. "Lead the way, Your Grace."

He led her to the floor and then he twirled her into the dance before she had time to change her mind, and she'd been close to doing so. The closer she'd stepped toward the light and the prying gazes of the ton she'd become increasingly more anxious. He'd been wise to take the decision away from her.

Julian was an amazing dancer, but that shouldn't have surprised her. Everything about him or that he did seemed to be perfect. "Now," he began. "This doesn't seem so bad does it, little one?"

At least he hadn't called her a mouse again… "No," she agreed. It was actually quite exhilarating. Lenora felt as if she was floating on air.

"I've always considered dancing to be too decadent to be done properly in a public forum," he began. "At least the sort I prefer."

She pushed her eyebrows together. "I'm not sure I follow…"

"I wouldn't expect you would," he replied secretively. "One day you might understand. Perhaps you'll tell me when you do." The corner of his lip turned upward almost…arrogantly. As if only he really understood the secrets of the world…

"I suspect, Your Grace, that our paths won't cross much in the coming years." The duke might be one of her cousin's friends, but she fully expected, at some juncture, to live on her own. Once she reached her majoring in a few months she planned to travel. Maybe to Italy… She hadn't fully decided yet. "We don't keep the same company and in time the little connections we have will dissipate."

"Perhaps," he agreed. "Time will tell I suppose." He twirled her around the floor expertly.

Lenora wouldn't ever forget this moment. She would likely never dance again, at least not like this. She was grateful she'd allowed the duke to convince her to participate. Afterward she'd likely find her way to her favorite corner to hide. In her darkest moments she'd be able to travel back to this waltz and recall it, and Julian fondly. If she believed she had a chance of something more with him… She shook that thought away. Loving him was a terrible idea and perhaps the only thing she regretted. This was a kindness, while out of character for him, but she shouldn't expect anything else from him.

The strands of the waltz ended and disappointment filled her. She'd tried to brush his request off at the start and now she never wanted the dance to end. The duke twirled her one last time around the floor and then led her to where their dance had begun. He bowed and kissed her gloved hand. "Thank you for your benevolence, my lady." His blue eyes twinkled with mischief. "And for being my protector when I need it."

She should be thanking him. He had awakened feelings in her she'd believed long buried. Her heart burst with happiness and affection for this man.

"You don't require my protection any more than you needed to dance with me." She frowned. Lenora still couldn't discern his motives for insisting on leading her in the waltz. "Either way the dance was lovely. I'm grateful I didn't insist against it."

He laughed lightly and shook his head. "Little mouse you're always so formal." Julian bowed again. "The pleasure was all mine." He glanced over his shoulder and then back at her. "Pardon me," he said. "I must attend to something important." His smile was bright and appeared genuine. "Enjoy the rest of your evening, my lady." With those words he spun on his heels and headed in the opposite direction.

Lenora smiled as she watched him wander off. She was starting to believe she had misjudged him. He'd been charming, as expected, but also kind and generous with his time. The duke hadn't been required to dance with her. No gentleman was. That made his attention all the more precious to her.

She wandered away from her favorite corner willingly for the first time all evening. Earlier didn't count because Julian had to coax her away from it. Perhaps she should leave the ballroom and explore the gardens. It was starting to become suffocating in the ballroom. Lenora's happiness was nearly bursting from within her. She hugged herself and twirled around as she made her way down the empty hallway leading to the balcony. There was a small staircase on the balcony that led down to the gardens.

Voices echoed back to her. Two male voices to be more precise and both were recognizable.

"Did she dance?" Her cousin asked. Why was Bennett so concerned about her dancing? Why couldn't he leave her to make her own decisions?

"Of course she did," Julian responded. "Do you doubt my ability to charm a woman?" He sounded so…disgusted. Was that because he had to dance with Lenora or because Bennett had doubted his ability? "I can coax any woman to do, well, anything," he boasted. "But a wallflower? That's not even a challenge."

She'd been jubilant until that moment. Now every amount of joy she'd held inside of her deflated in an instant. He'd appeared so kind earlier… How had she gotten it so wrong?

"Attention from you should have caught the notice of all the eligible gentleman in the room," Bennett said. "They'll want to know why the Duke of Ashley bothered with a wallflower. Soon she'll have more callers than she wants."

She didn't want any callers... A part of her hated her cousin for insinuating himself into her life this way. Why did he ask his friend to pay attention to her? Did he hate having her live with him that much? She'd thought they were closer than that...

"I've done you this favor," the duke said. "Don't ask it of me ever again." His tone was harsh and unyielding. It stabbed her in her fragile heart. She'd been on the brink of falling in love with him. The Duke of Ashley didn't deserve her affection. Lenora doubted he was worthy of any woman's love.

Tears stung her eyes and slid down her cheek. She brushed them away with a swipe of her fingertips. They wouldn't help her and they were as useless as her ability to read people. Lenora hardened her heart in that moment. She'd never play the fool again. It was time she learned to weave her way through society without letting another touch her soul again. She'd never be so easily duped again, but she had a lot to learn. There was one person who could teach her and she'd do whatever it took to convince her. That one person was the new Lulia Prescott—the gypsy Duchess of Clare...

With her decision made she rushed out of the

ballroom and walked all the way to the Holton townhouse. She'd need a good night of rest before she started her journey. Her first stop would be Tenby, Wales to visit with the duchess. After that she'd travel as planned. When she returned to London again she'd be an entirely different, better woman.

CHAPTER 1

April 1818

Lady Lenora St. Martin stared across the ballroom floor. It had been two years since she'd attended this particular matron's yearly ball. The Loxton ball had been when she'd finally been awakened to the possibilities life had to offer and when she realized Julian Everleigh, the Duke of Ashley was not only a rake, but also worthless. At least to her...

Two years working with the tutor that Lulia helped her find had changed her immensely. No longer was she the shy mouse who hovered in a corner. Now she was vibrant, strong, and determined to be the toast of the ton. She still had no real desire to marry. Lenora was content to become a rich spinster that created her own path and found happiness in something other than a man or a family.

This ball was her new start. The spring of her previous dreary life... Her dull brown hair was now streaked with gold from the time she spent in the Italian sun. Her drab hazel eyes sparkled with gold flecks she hadn't noticed before. Instead of an insipid white gown she'd dressed herself in the latest fashion. Her gown still had white worked through it, but it was also lined with blue satin and lace. The design emphasized her décolletage and hugged her curves. In short it was pure decadence.

"Are you sure you are prepared for this step," her escort asked. Luca Dragomir was a member of the royal family of the tiny island of Dacia, and the tutor Lulia had enlisted to assist her. Spending time in the warmth of Dacia, as well as, the Italian coast had helped heal her heart and find the strength she needed to change. Luca was handsome and confident, and not once since they became acquainted did he condescend to her. He'd treated her as if her opinion mattered…

She patted his arm and replied to his earlier question, "There will never be a more perfect time to return to London society." Lenora glanced up at him. His dark hair and sea-green eyes along with his tanned skin made him stand out against the dandies parading around the ballroom. The London ladies would swarm him and fawn over him. He was different and more or less, a prince. He was fifth in line to inherit the title, but that wouldn't matter to the marriage minded misses and their mothers.

"If you're certain…" He wound his arm with hers. "Then let's see where this leads us." Luca led her down the staircase that descended into the ballroom. Heads turned to stare at them as they slowly walked toward them all.

"I do believe we're making an entrance," he leaned down and whispered. "But is it a good one?" He lifted a brow.

As they continued their trek toward the bottom of the stairs a servant announced them. "Lady Lenora St. Martin and Prince Luca Dragomir, His Royal Highness of Dacia."

Once Luca's name was overheard the entire ballroom erupted. Lenora's lips tilted upward. "I do believe we're about to be approached," she said quietly. "Are you prepared to be courted?" It was her turn to lift a brow.

"Anything for a good cause," he replied cryptically. His lips twitched. "Do you have your dance card?"

She tapped her hand on the card tied to her wrist. "It's ready to be filled. Do you wish to claim your spot first?"

He lifted the card and jotted his name for the first dance of the evening. Then he bowed. "Until later, my lady." Luca left her alone at the edge of the dance floor. When the musicians started playing for the first dance he'd come back to retrieve her.

"That's quite an entrance," a male said from directly behind her. She recognized that voice. It was one she'd never forget and it still felt like a blade to her heart to hear it.

She turned to face him. "What are you implying?"

"I'm not…" He shook his head as if uncertain how to proceed. What novel idea. The Duke of Ashley was at a loss for words. He cleared his throat and started again, "I didn't mean to imply anything. I'm not going about this very well am I?" He bowed. "Let me introduce myself. I'm the Duke of Ashley."

He didn't recognize her… How interesting. This was something she could use against him if she chose to. She had been gone for a while, but she never once believed he'd forget her existence entirely. He was her cousin's friend after all. "I didn't realize it was acceptable to introduce oneself to someone," she said caustically. "Aren't you supposed to have a mutual acquaintance do the deed?"

"Well," he began. "I'm uncertain such a person exists. I don't recall seeing you at any of the balls of late." He motioned toward Luca who was surrounded by several ladies. "Or the interesting gentleman you arrived with."

All right this was becoming absurd. He might not recognize her but surely he had heard her name announced. Why was he not making the connection? Did he no longer speak to Bennett? She stared at him trying to discern his motives. "You truly don't know who I am do you?" He continued to meet her frank gaze and not once did it waver.

"Should I?" He lifted a brow.

Unreal… She let out an exasperated breath. If she'd been holding on to some delusional expectation that he secretly loved her…well it was a good thing she hadn't been because she'd be sorely disappointed now. He, of course, was as handsome as ever. The ducal god he presented to the world with golden blond hair and sinful blue eyes. "I don't suppose you would," she offered.

"Please allow me to rectify the slight I've given you." His voice held a bit of entreaty in it, but she didn't much care. She wasn't the same little mouse he'd lured out of the corner two years prior.

"That is unnecessary," she told him and started to walk away. He reached out and grabbed her arm. "Let go," she hissed under her breath. "I'm done with our conversation."

"I feel as if I should know you," he explained. "Your reaction and words says as much. How could I forget a vision like you?"

"Because you're a selfish arse," she replied scathingly. "Don't worry, Your Grace, I'm sure there is another lady here that would be willing to endure your charm." She yanked her arm free and sashayed away from him. Her lips tilted upward into a guileless smile. That had gone far better than she could ever have anticipated.

***

HE'D BEEN DISTRACTED BY HER BEAUTY AS SHE descended the stairs into the ballroom and had failed to hear her name as it was announced. Why didn't he recognize her? The more he talked to her he believed he should know her, but he couldn't place her. If she'd been around any society function of late surely he would have noticed her. How could he have not? She was a goddess and one not as pure white as the normal English miss. Her skin had a slight sun kissed bronze to it. She'd spent sometime outdoors of late. Which indicated she must not have been in England at all. Where had she come from? Perhaps the prince she'd arrived with would be able to answer some of his questions.

He wandered over to the crowd of ladies preparing to fawn over him. Julian had to admit to himself he wasn't used to another gentleman stealing his thunder. Usually they flocked toward him and he reveled in their attention. He liked to flirt and dance, but leave them all hanging in the end. Marriage wasn't on the table for him. Maybe one day, but he hoped that day was a long time coming. He'd witnessed first hand how a marriage could ruin a man's life. His father had foolishly fallen in love and paid the price for it. His mother had been the previous duke's undoing. She'd had numerous affairs and pushed his father away. She'd done her duty and bore him his heir. As far as the treacherous duchess was concerned she was free from any more obligations.

Maybe he could use the prince's popularity to his advantage. He moved closer to him and leaned down to whisper in one of the lady's ears nearby, "I never thought you'd be attracted by a princely title."

She sighed. "Do not be ridiculous. He's a friend nothing more. I had hoped to get a word with him, but it appears that won't be possible." The Duchess of Clare was a former Romany princess and her accent flowed through her words.

He lifted a brow. "You're friends with a prince? Why am I not surprised?" Julian chuckled lightly. "Are you acquainted with the female he arrived with as well?"

Maybe he wouldn't have to get any closer to the prince. He didn't really want to befriend him anyway. Something about the other man bothered Julian. He couldn't pinpoint exactly what it was though. He turned his attention back to Lulia, the Duchess of Clare.

"What is it?" he asked. In that moment he realized she never answered his earlier question. "You do know her, don't you?"

"Of course," she replied cryptically. "And so do

you." She sighed. "I had more faith in you than this. You really are a foolish man."

"Well," he said. "Who is she?" Julian couldn't keep the impatience out of his voice. He'd introduced himself to her, but she hadn't bothered to reciprocate. It irritated him a little he had to uncover the information on his own.

The duchess's throaty laughter echoed around him. Everyone near by stopped to glance back at them both, even the prince. That irritated Julian more than Lulia's mockery. She glanced at him with humor pouring out of her eyes. "You poor, poor sod," she said softly. "I shouldn't feel sorry for you, but once you realize what a fool you are you're going to kick yourself. I wish you luck."

"With what exactly?" He hated these cryptic discussions he'd been having since the moment the prince and his mystery lady arrived. Why wouldn't she just tell him who the lovely miss was? The lord knew he had no idea and he really could use some help.

"Recovering your head from your arse to start," the duchess nearly cackled with glee as she spoke.

"You always have a way with words." Julian rolled his eyes. "As usual this had been an riveting conversation. Tell me is your husband attending the ball today?" Perhaps Fin could help him with the lady's identity. If Lulia knew her surely he did as well.

The duchess shrugged. "He doesn't like society events. You know that."

He did. Fin didn't like leaving his townhouse unless absolutely necessary, but he also didn't like leaving Lulia either. "Is he in the card room then?" Fin had discovered a love of cards after a game at their club one day. "Perhaps I should join him there."

She shrugged. "Do as you please you always do." Then she turned away from him and walked toward the prince. The crowd parted for her and when she reached him he opened his arms and hugged her freely. That kind of affection wasn't the norm for society events. The ton would crucify them for it. Perhaps not though... Everyone knew how much Lulia and her husband adored each other. They didn't make any secret that their match was made with love. Not to mention they were all clamoring to know more about this enigmatic prince who landed at the Loxton ball.

Julian walked away from the crowd and headed to the ballroom. Lulia hadn't admitted that Fin could be found there, but he didn't see any reason not to check. He stopped once before he exited the ballroom and glanced back to his unknown lady. She was laughing at something another gentleman said. The strands of a waltz started to play indicating the dancing was about to start. The prince bowed to his admirers and went to the unidentified lady's side, then led her to the dance floor. They danced beautifully together and that irritated him even more. Something he'd never felt before washed over him—jealousy. He didn't like it one bit. He bit back the nauseating feeling and exited the room. Julian had to find Fin, and fast. This had to end sooner rather than later, because Julian hated being used as a pawn of any sort.

CHAPTER 2

Lenora sat in the sitting room of her cousin Bennett's townhouse staring at a nearby window. She was completely alone. Bennett and his wife, Katherine were at her horse farm and wouldn't return to London until after the birth of a foal they expected would be born soon. It gave her time to consider her own return to London and the feelings that kept rolling through her.

Her attendance at the ball had been a success. Luca had distracted many, but there were still several individuals that noted her arrival as well. Mostly gentlemen… Which had been their goal all along. The gentlemen and dandies would ensure her continued popularity. The ladies out of jealousy or their own desire to be the toast of the ton would flock to her side. Now that she made an appearance at her first ball of the season she needed to decide what invitations to accept.

The morning after the ball she'd been inundated with several personal invitations—to balls, dinner parties, soirees, and garden parties. Anything and everything imaginable was at her fingertips to accept or deny. Over night she'd become the toast of the ton, a diamond, the one lady they all clamored to have at their event. She wasn't a fool. Luca had played a large part in her success. Lenora couldn't rely on him indefinitely. She had spent the last two years improving herself and had to learn to actually like the person she'd turned into. While she didn't believe she owed anyone anything, she did want to be the best person she could be. That meant facing the world and not hiding from it.

"Pardon me, my lady," the butler said interrupting Lenora's thoughts. "Are you at home to callers?"

While the previous evening had gone well, she hadn't expected callers yet. She wasn't sure how to handle the situation. Who could possibly be at the townhouse for a visit? She made an internal decision and said, "Yes. Please have refreshments sent in as well."

The butler bowed. "Very well, my lady. I'll show your guest in then." He turned on his heels and exited the room.

Not long after the butler left a woman walked in. Lenora breathed a sigh of relief. She should have expected Lulia would come to visit her. After all she was the reason she'd broken out of her shell to begin with. "Your Grace," Lenora greeted. "Please join me."

"Enough with those formalities," Lulia said as she waved her hand in dismissal. She moved farther into the room and sat on a nearby settee. "You could have written to inform me of your plans to return to London. I trust your travels went well."

Lenora nodded. "My apologies. I wish we could have found a chance to speak last night. It was… unplanned." She frowned. When Luca suggested they return sooner than they had originally discussed she hadn't had time to write Lulia about it. "It seemed apropos for us to return at the start of the spring season. To…reveal the new me."

"I agree," Lulia said. "Luca was surrounded by quite a number of females at the ball so I didn't have a chance to speak with him either." She lifted her lips into a shrewd smile. "I did, however, have an interesting conversation with the Duke of Ashley."

"Oh?" Lenora lifted a brow. "I did as well. Pray tell, what did the duke have to say to you?"

She was still a little irritated at him. He'd been so charming, as usual, and hadn't recognized her at all. She still didn't understand how he could have not at least heard her name announced. He introduced himself, but didn't know who she was. There was something a bit odd about that. Perhaps she'd ask him about it the next time they crossed paths. There was no doubt in her mind that they would meet again. It was inevitable actually. She was staying at Bennett's townhouse until she found one of her own to purchase. Since she never intended to marry she'd need her own household. London was her home and she planned on settling down there at the first opportunity.

"He wanted to speak with Luca," Lulia began. "As you recall our favorite prince was preoccupied so he had to settle for a conversation with me." She brought her hands up and formed a steeple with them, then tapped her fingertips together. "He wanted to know more about you." She shook her head. "It's amazing how blind a man can be."

"I quite agree," she said. "He'll feel like a right idiot when he realizes who I am." She tapped her fingers on the arm of her chair. "I'm not sure what to do with this information. I never thought he'd fail to recognize me." Part of her acceptance of her life and who she was deep down inside was to finally have closure with what had happened between her and the Duke of Ashley. If he didn't even know who she was how could she achieve that? "Perhaps I should move on and forget about him entirely."

"Do you think you can do that?" Lulia asked. "It would be better for you if you could move on, but I don't believe that will be as easy as you want it to be."

A maid opened the door and wheeled in a teacart. "Pardon the interruption," she said. "I have brought the refreshments you requested, my lady." Two plates of food along with all the items they'd need for a proper tea were displayed on the cart.

Lulia licked her lips. "I'm glad you thought of this," she said and walked over to the teacart. "I'm starving."

Lenora rolled her eyes. "You're always hungry. If I'd realized you were my visitor I'd have requested extra food brought in. Help yourself." The last remark was unnecessary as Lulia was already filling a plate with pastries. The maid curtsied and left the room quietly.

She waited for Lulia to return to her seat and then answered her earlier question. "I'm uncertain if I can let go of my vendetta with the Duke of Ashley. I'll wait to make a decision."

"I think that's a wise choice," she replied between bites of her pastry.

After that they talked about pleasanter topics and genuinely enjoyed the afternoon. When Lulia left she penned a note and had it sent to Luca. She'd have to discuss their next public appearance with him sooner rather than later…

JULIAN STROLLED INTO HIS CLUB AND WANDERED over to the back room. He sat at a table and waited for one of the club's servants to bring him a drink. He'd been unable to uncover his mystery lady's identity. When he went in search of Fin in the card room it had been for naught. His duchess hadn't been lying. Her husband wasn't at the ball and wouldn't be able to provide Julian with any insight.

The servant brought over a glass of brandy and

set it in front of Julian. "Will you require anything else, Your Grace?"

"No that will be all," Julian said. "Actually bring me the entire bottle of brandy." He wanted to drink until he was completely foxed. Julian hated failing at anything.

He downed the contents of his glass and set it down. The servant brought the bottle over and refilled his glass, then sat the brandy decanter on the table. Julian sipped on his drink slower this time.

"What has you drinking already," a male asked. Julian glanced up and met his friend, the Earl of Northesk's gaze.

"Northesk," he greeted him. "I didn't realize you were back from convalescing in the country. How are your wife and son?" The Earl of Northesk's son had to be around a year old now. Julian tended to lose track of time regarding the age of children. He just didn't care enough…

"My family is doing all right," Northesk answered him. "You didn't answer my question."

"Do you think I need a reason to drink?" Julian lifted a brow and lifted his glass of brandy, then took a long sip. "Any day is a good day to imbibe too much and have a jolly good time. Sit and have a glass yourself."

All of his friends were happily wed. It was almost…disgusting. He spent far too much time on his own now. Julian didn't understand why they had all decided to fall in love and shackle themselves to one woman for the rest of their days. Love, in his opinion, was toxic. It changed a man into someone else entirely. Julian didn't have any desire to be anything other than the person he was. No woman was going to change him. His current obsession aside…a woman wouldn't control him. Ever.

"I'll pass on the brandy," Northesk replied. "But I will join you." He pulled out a chair and sat at the table with him. "Have you heard from Holton?"

The marquess was in the country at his wife's horse farm. They were there more than they were in London most days. "I have not. Is there any reason you need to speak with him?"

"No," Lord Northesk shook his head. "I heard a rumor his cousin, Lady Lenora returned to London. Diana is acquainted with her and she want's to pay a call on her. Neither one of us is certain where she's settled at."

Julian frowned. He'd forgotten about the Marquess of Holton's cousin. She hadn't been seen for a couple of years. The lady was a complete flower and a shy little mouse. He'd danced with her once as a favor to Holton. She'd been inconsequential to him and he'd dismissed her as unimportant and forgot about her existence. He tended to do that often. Perhaps he should change the way he treated people… Julian could be a bit of an arse and leaned toward selfish tendencies more often than not.

He ran his finger over the rim of his glass. "I wouldn't know anything about his cousin's whereabouts," he answered. "I barely knew the girl. Hell I doubt I'd recognize her if she walked in front of me." Her features were a little hazy in his memories. She had brown hair…and that was all he could recall. He really was an arse… If he crossed paths with Lady Lenora again he'd apologize for being a conceited moron. No one should be treated so badly. He drained the contents of his glass…again.

The earl shook his head. "You shouldn't spend so much time alone, my friend. You're in quite a dark mood."

"I'm not certain I know what you mean," Julian replied evasively.

"Yes, you do," the earl said firmly. "But I won't push. I know how you get at this time of the year.

You forget we've known each other since Eton. You have no secrets from me."

Julian doubted that. Though Northesk did know more about him than most people. The Earl of Northesk and the Marquess of Holton were his two closest friends. They tended to tell each other everything—most of the time. If he asked Northesk to help him uncover his mystery lady's identity he'd probably help him. Something held Julian back from asking though. He didn't want to involve his friend for some reason and he didn't quite know why.

"That may be true," Julian began. "But I don't particularly feel like rehashing old wounds at the moment." Instead he refilled his glass and proceeded to swallow the brandy in quick gulps. At this rate he'd be foxed in minutes rather than hours.

"All right," Northesk agreed. "But if you change your mind…"

"I won't," Julian interrupted him. "Some things are best forgotten." He'd just need something else to help distract him from the demons of his past…like his mystery lady and the prince she brought home with her.

"Have it your way," the earl replied. "You always do. I'll leave you to your brandy." Northesk came to his feet. "I'm going to go home to my family. If you want company you know where to find me." With those words he turned and left Julian alone.

His friend meant well, but Julian didn't want to darken his doorstep with the evils of his past. It was best he sorted it all out on his own, but first he fully intended to go through the entire bottle of brandy and maybe another before he departed the club.

CHAPTER 3

Lenora was restless. She didn't want to stay cooped up on her cousin's townhouse for another moment. Luca hadn't responded to her missive and it was making her nervous. He was supposed to help her. How could she move forward with her plan if he wasn't there to help her implement it?

Perhaps a little bit of exercise would help her. She could go for a stroll at Rotten Row. It would benefit her twofold. It gave her a reason to move around and stop thinking too hard. In addition to that it would ensure she was seen by the beau monde. The Duke of Ashley had noticed her. She'd keep his attention on her and get the revenge she desired. She *would* continue on the path she'd carved for herself—the mysterious new Lady Lenora St. Martin. Beautiful, charismatic, and sophisticated enough to attract the attention of a prince.

She stood and walked to the foyer. Her cloak hung on a hook near the door. She could easily don it and be on her way, but she couldn't go alone. It wouldn't look right… Her maid could accompany her, but then what? Would the ton scoff at her for her lack of companions? Lenora shook that thought away. It wouldn't aid her cause. She had to stop second-guessing herself and just do whatever she wanted. She was no longer an ingénue. She'd left that naïve girl behind and became something better.

"Mary," Lenora called for the maid.

After several seconds the maid came to the foyer. She curtsied and said, "Yes, my lady."

"I am going for a walk and I require you to attend me."

"Yes, my lady," she replied. "When are we to depart?"

Lenora frowned. Mary wasn't the brightest girl in the house. It was part of the reason she wished for her to accompany her. "I'd like to leave at this very moment," she informed her. "Please go tell the housekeeper you're going to be with me and hurry back without delay."

"Very well," Mary said in a congenial tone. Then she turned on her heels and headed in the direction that the housekeeper could be found.

While she awaited the maid's return Lenora pulled her cloak off the hook and put it on. She tied the ribbon at her neck and then donned her bonnet. The sun would be shining bright and she didn't want to freckle her skin. As she was securing the bonnet Mary returned ready for their stroll in Hyde Park.

"Mrs. Benson has been notified," Mary said. "And she said to tell you to enjoy your walk."

Lenora smiled. The housekeeper had always been one of her biggest supporters. She had missed Mrs. Benson while she'd been away. It was good to be home where she was loved. Even if it was the same place that she'd been pushed to the shadows time and time again. "Come, Mary," she said as she headed toward the door. "The sun won't wait for us. It'll set on schedule whether we are there to enjoy it or not."

They exited the townhouse and started walking toward Hyde Park. Mary stayed quiet as they strolled along and that suited Lenora just fine. She didn't particularly want to participate in small talk. She'd rather have had Luca with her though.

Why hadn't he answered her?

It bothered her more than she wanted to admit. She needed more than to just to discuss the public appearances together. Lenora also wanted to ask his advice on some properties she was considering. There was a townhouse in Mayfair and one on the outskirts of London. The townhouse would probably be more manageable if she intended to live alone. The house would be so big and lonely all by herself. Still she wanted to make the most economical and sound choice. For that she'd have to dig deep into the specifics of each property and Luca would make a good person to discuss it all with. She trusted his opinion.

They reached the edge of the park. It was bustling with activity and Lenora suddenly didn't want to be seen by any of them. She held her shoulders high and kept moving forward though. It wouldn't do her any good to arrive and then hide at the first opportunity. She'd take a few turns on the walking path and then find her favorite spot in the park to rest and be by herself. She'd rounded the path twice before someone dared to speak to her.

"Lady Lenora," a matron greeted her. "It's so

good to see you back here in England. Traveling has suited you."

"Thank you Lady Marvelle," she said. "It was wonderful and it is good to be home. There is no place like England."

"Too true," Lady Marvelle responded. "I trust you're home to stay." She leaned a little close and whispered loudly, "You're not going to let that handsome prince whisk you away forever are you?"

That was Lady Marvelle's way of trying to get information that everyone wanted. The gossips were probably dying to know more about Luca. She couldn't really blame them. He was a handsome devil… "Prince Luca is a wonderful man and so charming," she told Lady Marvelle. "I might not be able to resist."

Lady Marvelle's cheeks reddened a little and she fanned herself. "Oh to be as young as you are again." She smiled. "If you do fall in love with the handsome prince no one would blame you, my dear. But do take care. I'd hate for you to be left with a broken heart."

"I will," she assured the matron. "My heart couldn't survive such a blow." A second time…

"Enjoy your stroll," Lady Marvelle said. "I see Lady Silverton and I must speak to her. It was a pleasure seeing you again." With those words Lady Marvelle flitted off.

After she was out of sight Lenora left the main path and headed toward the small pond at the back of the park. There were usually ducks there at this time of the day. She could sit on the grass under a tree and admire them as she had in the past. It sounded like a much better time than walking the path of Rotten Row.

JULIAN SAT ON HIS HORSE OBSERVING THE inhabitants of Hyde Park. He'd stayed away from the main path on Rotten Row not particularly wanting to be seen by anyone. There wasn't anyone in the park he wanted to talk to anyway. He was in a surly mood. The lady from the other night hadn't made an appearance and he still had no idea who she was. He didn't understand how he couldn't uncover her name.

He didn't even know why he was still in the park. It would probably be better for everyone if he just went home and sulked in private, but that idea didn't sit well with him. He didn't like the idea of being cooped up inside his house. Julian couldn't recall the last time he had been this stir crazy. He caught a glimpse of a lady walking away from the path. She wore a blue muslin-walking gown and had a matching bonnet covering her hair. He was intrigued enough to press his knee into the side of his horse and gesture for it to follow in her direction. Julian had a gut feeling and he always listened to his instincts. Could this be the lady he'd hoped to find?

After he was away from Rotten Row he slowed his horse down to a complete stop, then dismounted. He led the horse by the reins and walked silently in the direction the lady had gone. Julian stopped short when he saw a small pond in the distance. The lady sat nearby with her bonnet down hanging around her neck by the loosened ribbons. It rested against her back leaving her dark hair exposed. She tilted her head back basking in the sunshine.

He was mesmerized. She was so bloody beautiful…

Julian shook himself out of his transfixion and tied his horse to a nearby tree, then headed in her direction. There was no doubt in his mind that this was the lady he sought. Suddenly he was nervous.

Julian had never felt anything like it in his entire life. What should he even say to her?

He moved closer to her keeping his footsteps light and even. What was she doing out here alone. Didn't she even have a maid with her?

"Mary," she called. "Is that you? Come join me by the pond."

"It's not Mary," he admitted. Who was Mary? Her maid perhaps?

She turned suddenly and met his gaze. Her lips turned down and she narrowed her gaze. "Oh," she said caustically. "It's you."

That sharp tone of hers took him back a little bit but he wouldn't let it detract him. He had a purpose and he would see it through. She could slash him with her razor tongue but he would prevail in the end. "Yes," he agreed. "It is most definitely me." He flashed her what he considered to be his most charming smile. "Do you mind if I join you."

She rolled her eyes in the most unladylike manner and blew out an exasperated breath. "If you insist."

The lady turned away from him and focused her attention on the pond. She glanced briefly around her. Probably looking for the elusive Mary.

Julian was going to take advantage of the missing maid. He sat down beside her. "What are we looking at?"

She turned her attention to him and gave him the most oblivious look he'd ever seen. "Have you never seen a pond before, Your Grace?"

"Of course," he said easily. She could be as acerbic as she wanted to be. He fully intended to be charming and kind. "But I thought perhaps there was something more miraculous to see considering the amount of attention you're bestowing upon it."

She closed her eyes and remained silent for several heartbeats. He enjoyed staring at her unobserved for that amount of time. She was the most ethereal woman he'd ever seen and he couldn't believe he'd never made her acquaintance before now. Still, there was something familiar about her and he couldn't discern what it was. Her eyelids fluttered open like a butterfly unfurling its wings and flashing its beauty to the world. "Do you not ever bask in something beautiful just for the sake of enjoying the pleasure of its existence?" She lifted a perfectly arched brow. "I've always found this spot to be serene and perfect. No one ever really comes over here. So I can sit here and just…be."

He'd been basking in her beauty a moment ago so he could answer honestly, "Yes," he told her. "I have appreciated something exquisite upon occasion." Like her…

"Tell me, my lady," he said. "Are you ever going to grace me with the knowledge of your name?"

She laughed and it was music to his ears. "I'm not denying you anything, Your Grace." She stood and glanced down at him. "You have already been introduced to me several times. Perhaps you should do something about your faulty memory."

What? He couldn't have been introduced to her before. He'd… Surely he'd remember her? She started to walk away and he scrambled to his feet. He couldn't let her leave without at least getting a hint to who she was. Her maid came wandering over then and preventing him from keeping her there much longer.

"Wait," he said. "Can you at least take pity on me."

"Oh," she said turning to meet his gaze. "Trust me, Your Grace. I've done nothing but take pity on you."

With those words she rushed to her maids side and continued walking away from him. Now more than ever he was determined to uncover her identity. If they'd been introduced in the past he could narrow his search. She wasn't new to town and that gave him something to work with. Now all he would have to do is make a list of all the young ladies who had been away from society for a short time…

CHAPTER 4

It had been a sennight since Julian had crossed paths with his mysterious lady. He had all but given up on her attending any society functions or at least the ones he'd bothered to make an appearance at. Most of them he walked in did a few loops around the ballroom or garden depending on the location, then once he realized she wasn't there he promptly left. In most soirees or balls he didn't even do that much and these ones the hostess was lucky if he bothered to make their regards or take their leave. He just didn't care about what they thought about them or their social gathering. Julian had gone for one reason and when that reason wasn't in attendance he promptly departed. Yes, it was rude, but he was a man on a mission. He hadn't been intrigued by a woman in well, ever.

Now that he'd left an afternoon tea party. God. Where do the society ladies come up with these things? What happened to having a decent cup of tea at home without the niceties of small talk? Not that he partook in an afternoon tea much, but still… It was ridiculous. What he needed was a good cup of brandy or several. Which was why after he left Lady Hickam's tea party he went straight to his club. He'd been at White's far more than he liked to admit lately.

He strolled into White's and headed straight to the card room. There weren't usually too many gentlemen there at this time of day, but he did hope he could find someone to help keep him entertained. Turned out he was in luck. Not only were there some gentlemen there about to set up a game of Faro, the Royal Prince of Dacia had sat down at the table. He might not have been able to find his mystery lady, but he had found the prince who had escorted her.

Julian headed over to the table and took an empty chair. The good thing about faro was that any number of individuals could play. So the gentlemen couldn't turn him away because their table was full. He fully intended to take advantage of that. It would give him a prime opportunity to gain the measure of Prince Luca. "Hello," he greeted them. "Lord Aderton." He nodded at the earl. "Lord Midvale." Julian smiled at his friend. The viscount had been at Oxford with him. "Mind if I join you?" He purposely ignored the prince. He didn't want to overplay the hand fate had dealt him.

Midvale nodded at him. "Of course," he said jovially. "Your always welcome Ashley." He gestured toward the prince. "Have you met Prince Luca?"

"I've not had the pleasure," he replied smoothly. "What brings you to London?" Julia had to hold back how eager he was to meet the man, finally. "What country are you from again?" He would not give the man the satisfaction of realizing exactly how much, or more accurately, how little Julian had been able to uncover about him.

"It's a small nation," Luca said in a cultured tone. "Not many have visited or even heard of it."

Julian scrunched his eyebrows together. "Admittedly I didn't venture far on my supposed world tour when I finished at Oxford, but I wouldn't say I'm ignorant of the world's geography."

Prince Luca's lips turned upward into a sneer. "I didn't mean to insult your intelligence, Your Grace."

So the prince knew who he was. Midvale hadn't used his title when he had introduced them. If that was what you could call what Midvale had actually done. How much did the prince know about Julian? He hated that the other man had more information on him than Julian could claim to have on the prince. He would have to find a way to even the playing field. "Think nothing of it." Julian waved a hand dismissively. It hadn't escaped his notice the prince still hadn't given him the location of his monarchy. "I'm sure once you tell me your country's name I'll be able to recall it."

His sneer had turned into a smirk. Julian was really starting to dislike the prince. "Dacia is an island in the Mediterranean."

Julian would have to glance at a few maps when he returned home. He didn't recall any islands with that name. He should have already done so. Why hadn't he? "I see," he replied amicably. "So how are you enjoying London?"

They all took their seats at the table. One of the

servants at White's was acting as the dealer. He shuffled the fifty-two-card deck and set the game up. Julian nonchalantly placed his bet and waited for everyone else to do the same. After the cards were all in place and the bets were made the prince glanced his way and responded to his question. "I've found London pleasant. The ladies have all been particularly inviting and some of the gentlemen have opened their doors as well. This club of yours is interesting. I'll have to speak to my brother upon my return about opening something similar in Dacia."

Julian would not roll his eyes. "You have a brother?" He lifted a brow. "Which one of you is in line to rule?"

"I'm more than happy to leave that task to Nicolai," he said smoothly. "As second in line I have more freedom and it gives me leave to travel." His lips tilted upward into a wicked grin. "Plus I can court as many women as I like until I find the right one. Nicolai must marry a bride chosen for him."

Julian had to admit he wouldn't want his wife to be handpicked for him either. "Do you have a lady in mind to be your intended?" He hoped it wasn't the mystery lady he wanted to court himself.

"I do," he said. "She's a true English beauty. It's

just a matter of convincing her I'm her perfect match."

Julian gritted his teeth. They weren't affianced yet. He still had a chance to convince the dark haired beauty he was the better choice. First he had to find her and discover her name. He continued to play Faro but his heart wasn't in it. He lost badly and then stood to excuse himself. "Gentlemen," he nodded at them all as he spoke. "It has been a pleasure but I must beg your leave. I have a prior engagement at the theater." He didn't wait for them to respond. Julian turned on his heels and exited the room and then out of White's. He had to go home and prepare for another social function of sorts—the theater.

Lenora strolled into the theater with Luca at her side. They were going to watch some Shakespearean play. She couldn't recall which one… Luckily she had the use of her cousin Bennett's box for the night. Luca had finally answered her missive. It had nearly driven her mad while she awaited his reply. This was their first outing together since that first ball.

"Everyone is looking at you," he whispered in her ear.

She lifted her lips upward into a satisfied smirk. "No, Luca dear. They're staring at both of us. We make quite the striking pair don't you think?

Luca met her gaze and returned her grin. "I do believe you're correct, darling." The walked past several gawking members of the ton and headed straight to Bennett's box. "What are we being subjected to tonight?"

She shrugged. "Besides gossip and innuendo?" Lenora laughed. "Though I suppose those will be rampant in the play at some point as well."

He chuckled. "At the very least you're correct." Luca nodded to the theater at large. "The audience will definitely share rumors and lies in tandem."

Luca pushed open the curtain and allowed her to enter before him. She started when she found Bennett in the box with his wife Katherine. "Cousin," she greeted. "I hadn't realized you returned to London already."

"We arrived earlier today," he glanced past her at Luca. "Who is this?"

Bennett stood and Lenora hugged him quickly in greeting and then hugged Katherine as well. "It's good to see you both." She ignored his earlier question for the moment.

"Why didn't you write and inform us you were returning?" Bennett wasn't going to let any of it go.

She sighed. "I didn't know I was ready to come home until the last minute." She motioned toward Luca. "Prince Luca was kind enough to accompany me back."

Bennett glared at him. "I'm sure he was."

This wasn't going well at all, but then she hadn't figured Bennett would accept the choices she'd made. She smiled at him and acted as flippant as possible. It hurt that he didn't believe she could take care of herself. Though she couldn't really blame him. Not entirely anyway… She had been a mouse that hid in the corner before she'd left. Bennett would have to become acquainted with the new her. "Don't be cross," she said cajolingly. "We're all here to see a play and lucky for us, we get to do it together."

Bennett frowned but conceded. He turned his attention to Luca and greeted him as amicably as Lenora expected he would. "Thank you for looking out for my cousin." He motioned to the seats in the box. "Please join us."

"It was my pleasure to assist Lady Lenora," Luca replied. "She's a wonderful woman."

Bennett gritted his teeth but didn't respond to Luca's jab. Instead he took his seat next to his wife and kept silent. His cheeks had taken a heady glow to it that indicated he was quite mad. He wouldn't cause a scene at the theater, but she fully expected he would have a row with her later. When his anger and disapproval was unleashed he'd discover soon after she was no longer the meek young lady he'd been able to maneuver the way he thought best. She could make up her own mind and decide which direction she should take with her life. Lenora didn't require a man to dictate to her.

Luca escorted her over to her seat and assisted her into it. He then sat on her left. Just when she thought everything was settled for the rest of their outing the curtains parted and Julian walked in. She cursed under her breath. What were the chances he'd come into Bennett's box. He hadn't noticed her. His attention was completely on her cousin.

"Holton," he greeted. "I didn't know you were back in town. I saw you enter from my box and had to come by before the play starts."

Her cousin's face lit up at Julian's arrival. Why wouldn't it? They were close friends and it was one of the only reasons that Lenora was acquainted with Julian. She really didn't want him to notice her while Bennett was around. Then the jig would be up. He'd realize who she was and that easy-going façade he displayed around her would return. The one that was polite but distant. Lenora hated it. She rather enjoyed the anonymity she'd had around him.

"We've only just returned," Bennett told Ashley. The friendly tone Bennett saved for his closest friends and family was evident in his voice. "We'll only be in London for a short while. Why don't you stay here in my box? Or do you have something pressing in yours you must attend to?" What Bennett implied with that question was Julian might have his mistress in his box. It wasn't unusual for him to do something of that nature. She did her best not to snicker at her cousin's implication.

Thus far, Julian hadn't noticed her or Luca. She sat on the edge of her seat, but kept her face forward toward the stage. If he happened to glance in her direction she didn't want him to catch her staring at him. Her heart beat heavily in her chest. Waiting. For him. He would notice. It would just be a matter of time and then…

Julian's rich throaty chuckle echoed toward her.

"I'm alone," he said honesty echoing through his tone. "I've been rather tame of late. I…" his voice trailed off and Lenora's lips tilted upward when she realized he'd noticed her. He was silent a moment before saying, "Yes, I do think I'll stay here with you."

He'd definitely noticed… Now the question was. What would he do next?

CHAPTER 5

When Julian reluctantly headed to the theater earlier he had no idea he'd find his elusive lady sitting in the Marquess of Holton's box. Sure, she was also in the seat directly next to Prince Luca, but he could work with that. She was there and more importantly, acquainted with Holton. That meant he had to have met her before. His brain just wouldn't shake the information free.

Holton's box had six seats. He could sit next to Katherine, the marquess's wife or he could take the seat next to the lady he'd hoped to get to know better. To him it wasn't much of a choice. He liked the marchioness well enough, but he didn't want to spend the entire play by her side. Besides he would have been more difficult to get to the seat next to Katherine. Where as he could easily slide into the other seat and be directly behind his friend. If they wished to speak at all it would be as simple as Holton turning to face him.

He slid into the seat next to her. She turned to face him and her lips tilted upward into a serene smile. Julian wasn't sure what he'd expected her to do, but it hadn't been this easy acceptance. Though what else could she possibly have done? Throw a fit and demand he move? That would have caused a scene and no one wanted to become gossip fodder.

"Good evening," he said and then glanced at the prince. "Your Highness I thought you'd stay at White's longer. Were you not winning before I left?"

Luca's lips twitched amusement evident in his eyes. "Indeed," he replied. "But I always keep my promises and I gave my word to the lovely lady I'd escort her tonight."

"And I thank you for it." She smiled at the prince adoringly. "I can always rely upon you when I am in need."

Julian's stomach soured as he listened to them. He had to figure out how to separate them. Prince Luca said all the right things, but Julian didn't believe for a second that he was truly in love with her. He was only going through the motions and the lady basked in the falsehood. "How wonderful for you," he said but it grated to say even that much.

"It is." Her tone was light and happy sounding.

"The play is starting soon," Holton interjected. "As enlightening as your conversation is can you hold it until intermission."

The marquess had always been a stickler for the rules. Only his wife could ruffle his feathers and get him to bend a little. Katherine placed her hand on his arm and said, "Don't be difficult dear. Let Lenora talk with her two suitors. We still have a few moments until the play begins."

Holton glared at her. "I doubt Ashley is courting my cousin and I'm not sure I like the company she's keeping these days."

Julian felt as if someone had punched him in his solar plexus. She couldn't be Lady Lenora St. Martin. He would have recognized her. He whipped his head around and met her gaze. Her lips tilted upward into a wanton smile. Bloody hell… It was Lady Lenora. Now he felt like a complete idiot. How could he have not realized who she was? More importantly, when had she turned into a gorgeous vixen?

"Your wife is correct," Lady Lenora announced.

"The Duke of Ashley would never court me. He's never noticed I existed long enough to realize I'm a woman let alone one of marriageable age." She smiled. "But that's all right since I don't wish him to bother. I've set my sights on a more attainable goal."

What the hell was that supposed to mean? He'd noticed her. How could he have failed to? She was the cousin of one of his best friends. They'd been introduced and he'd even danced with her…once. He couldn't be blamed for not courting her sooner. He hadn't wanted a wife and he wouldn't have encouraged a young lady for anything. That was why he stayed away from most society functions. He would rather find his entertainments in his club or a den of iniquity. There were not innocent misses to be found in those types of places. Lady Lenora on the other hand had always been untouchable. That was why he'd kept her at a distance. If he'd been overly flirtatious or led her to believe he wanted more and then didn't come up to scratch… That would have ruined his friendship with Holton.

Even now he had to stop and consider what courting her might mean. If things went sour Holton wouldn't look upon him in a favorable light. Julian didn't have many friends and he didn't want to lose one of the few good ones he had over a woman. He had to be dam sure he wanted her before he took another step.

He nodded in her direction and said, "It's good to have goals. What is it you hope to achieve?" He lifted a brow. "Haven't you been traveling for a couple of years now?" She sure had blossomed in that intervening time…

"A great many things," she said evasively. "I learned a lot in my travels, but mostly I discovered what I want for myself and who I am underneath."

"She's quiet intelligent," the prince interjected. "We've had many discussions about literature, philosophy, and the sciences. She has some ideas regarding architecture that I might consider utilizing when I return home."

"Oh?" Lady Lenora was a regular bluestocking by the sounds of it. "I didn't realize you are so…"

"Intelligent?" She lifted a brow.

His lips twitched. "That wasn't the word I was searching for." He wanted to uncover all of her secrets. Julian decided in that instant that he would indeed court Lady Lenora. She was his match in every way. "I was going to say that diverse in your interests. I've always known you to have a superior intellect."

He wasn't sure how she would have responded to that. The curtains on the stage opened and the Shakespearean play had started. He'd have to wait until later to spar with her again. He was looking forward to the barbs she'd throw his way too. Julian had grown a little perverse in his maturity.

INTERMISSION. LENORA HADN'T BEEN ABLE TO FOCUS on the play. The entire time she'd been overly aware of Julian sitting next to her. He had been a perfect gentleman the entire time. She hated it. Why couldn't he be an overbearing arse? Then she could continue to hate him. Truthfully he hadn't ever done anything horrible to her. He'd just been dismissive of her and what feelings she had.

It wasn't his fault she'd stupidly fallen in love with him. She'd fled England to learn how to be independent and grow a sense of self-assurance. She'd done both, but her heart still skipped a beat at a glance from this man or the sound of his rich baritone. There had never been anything romantic between them, but oh she'd wanted there to be. She desired so much from him and been denied at every turn. After that one dance she thought perhaps he'd finally noticed her. That he might come to love her. She'd been wrong.

"Do you want to go for a stroll and stretch your legs?" Luca. He was being the attentive escort he promised to be. She didn't want to take a walk with him though. She would rather stay near Julian. How pathetic she was… Lenora could spend years abroad and still she'd be a fool for one man.

She shook her head and said, "No. Go ahead if you'd like to move around a little before the intermission is over."

"If you don't mind…" He lifted a brow questioningly.

"I promise," she reassured him. "I'll be fine. Go."

Julian had already left as soon as the curtains closed. He had exited with her cousin fast on his heels. Bennett probably wanted to interrogate the duke. She didn't know what questions her cousin might have, but she was certain he had a few. He'd had that look on his face. Once Luca left the box Katherine came to sit by her. She placed her hand on Lenora's. "Do you wish to talk about it?"

"No…yes…" She nibbled on her bottom lip. "I…"

"You don't have feelings for the prince,"

Katherine supplied. "At least not those of the romantic variety."

She shook her head slowly. "Luca is a friend," she admitted.

"But you're in love with the Duke of Ashley," Katherine stated the problem aloud.

"Am I that obvious?" Her heart thundered in her chest and the beating echoed in her eardrums. Was Julian able to see through her carefully crafted façade?

"No," Katherine answered her. "But I've known you for a while now and I witnessed first hand how you gazed upon him years ago. It isn't clear now. You're much better at hiding your feelings." She paused and then added, "I'm not so sure that's a good thing or not. Did Julian do something to hurt you in the past."

"Not purposefully…"

"Intentionally or not that doesn't make it hurt any less," Katherine stated.

Lenora was more than well aware of that particular fact. "No it doesn't…" Her voice trailed off as she recalled that fateful night she had realized how insignificant she'd been to the Duke of Ashley. It hadn't been her best night.

"What do you want now?" Katherine asked

softly. "Do you hope he'll notice you? Marry you?" She tilted her head to the side. "Or are you just hoping he'll leave you alone?"

Lenora wasn't so sure how to answer that question. "When I first stepped foot back in London I wanted to make him hurt as much as he'd hurt me."

"And now?" Katherine inquired.

"I'm not so sure," she admitted. "He's been so attentive and charming. I'd like to say nothing like he was before but that's not right. He's always been that way."

"Just not with you."

Katherine's statement described exactly what the problem with her situation was. He'd never been this attentive with her before. How could she trust him now? What if he was toying with her? "I have my doubts…"

"Of course you do," Katherine said. "How could you not? The path to love is never an easy one. I know that better than anyone. Bennett and I didn't fall at each other's feet. We fought every step of the way until we had no choice but to admit that we loved each other."

Lenora recalled that time. Bennett complained about the lady who owned a horse farm constantly back then. She'd known who Katherine was, but she hadn't been a close friend of hers. Lulia had been the one to guide Lenora and teach her how to love herself. The gypsy turned duchess had a way of inspiring a person to be better than they thought they could be. She owed Lulia a lot. If not for her she might not have been brave enough to leave England in the first place. "But you found your way to each other. In the end that is what matters."

"That is true," Katherine answered. "Julian might surprise you. He does seem interested…"

"He didn't know who I was," Lenora admitted. "He didn't recognize me and that made me a mystery he needed to solve. Now that he knows I fear he'll lose interest."

"I don't think you're giving him enough credit." Katherine frowned. "Julian isn't as hard hearted as you're making him out to be. Sure maybe you were a bit of a challenge at first, but that doesn't mean he's done pursuing you. I'm willing to bet he won't find you so easy to fall at his feet now either. Or am I wrong?"

Lenora shook her head. "No. I'm not the naïve girl I used to be."

"Then enjoy the attention and wait to decide later." She smiled encouragingly. "The duke isn't the same man you left behind either. Give him a chance and maybe, just maybe, you'll discover he feels the same way you do."

Lenora wasn't so certain about it as Katherine was, but she was willing to at least keep her options open. If Julian loved her... She couldn't imagine what that might be like. To have him and be loved by the man she'd always adored... She'd give just about anything for that. Katherine was right about one thing. She owed it to herself to at least explore the possibility. Maybe she should stop pushing Julian away and discover exactly what he hoped to gain by courting her.

CHAPTER 6

The Silverly ball was the event of the season. Anyone who was anyone clamored for an invitation and no one turned down the invite once they received it. That made the ball the single most crushing ball of the season. Lenora hated every second of it. She'd attended hoping that Julian would as well. If he truly meant to court her then he'd want to attend a function for that purpose.

But he hadn't come…

She'd listened carefully to all the announcements made and he wasn't in any of the arrivals. Lenora hated that she'd been waiting for him the entire time only to be disappointed in the end. Why did she keep doing this to herself? Julian had only pursued her because she was an enigma. Now that allure was gone he'd lost interest. She didn't know why she'd expected anything else.

"Do you wish to dance?" Luca asked.

Lenora didn't know what she wanted anymore. She'd thought she wanted to have Julian notice her and then break his heart the way he'd broken hers. She'd realized too late that she wasn't that petty and what she really desired was his love. Now she wasn't so sure she even had a chance of love with him at all. She wanted it…craved it, but it still remained elusive. If he were standing before her now she still might not be able to openly accept him. She sighed. "I'm not in much of a dancing mood."

He lifted a brow. "Then what sort of mood are you in?"

"A petulant one," she admitted. "I'm sorry. I'm being a brat."

She glanced around the room and stopped when she saw a row of wallflowers hugging the walls. There was a shy pretty girl in the corner Lenora used to occupy. She had rich auburn hair and a delicate heart shaped face. In a few years she'd be gorgeous and perhaps she'd lose that edge of innocence about her as Lenora had. She hoped the girl wouldn't end up with a heart as shattered as

Lenora's. She narrowed her gaze and studied the girl.

"What has your attention now?"

She gestured with a shake of her head at the wallflower. "Do you see that girl in the corner?"

"The red haired waif?" He scrunched his eyebrows together. "What of her."

"That used to be me," she said softly. "It feels like another lifetime now, but that was my corner. I hid there and most of the time I prayed no one noticed me. The other part of the time I craved to be noticed. At least long enough to be pulled on to the dance floor. Oh how I loved dancing and no one ever asked me."

"What would you have me do?" He raised a brow. "Ask the young lady to dance?" He tilted his head to the side and studied the red haired innocent. "She looks barely eighteen and as innocent as a newborn babe."

Lenora smiled. "That she does." She met Luca's gaze. "And yes, go ask her to dance. But first you need to be introduced. Come with me."

His mouth opened and closed several times but he did as she asked. They crossed the room and stopped in front of the young lady. Luca didn't realize that Lenora knew exactly who the young miss was. She should be the most sought after new debutante in the room, and yet, she'd become the most ignored. Lade Evelina Davenport was the daughter of the Duke of Livingstone and had a huge dowry. Once the fortune hunters realized she was out they'd flock to her side. Then she'd hide even more than she was now. She clearly couldn't discern a way to handle being out in society.

She stopped and greeted her, "Lady Evelina, it's been too long since we last spoke. I didn't realize you were ready for your come out already."

Her eyes widened as she glanced from Lenora to Luca. "I…" She cleared her throat. "My come out ball was a fortnight past."

"How wonderful," Lenora exclaimed. "You must have been so excited."

"I…was," she said with a hint of uncertainty. Lady Evelina swallowed hard. Her eyes were as big as saucers. She clearly hadn't thought anyone would pay her any mind. Lenora understood that feeling well. She'd hidden in the corner often enough.

"I'd like you to meet my dear friend," she gestured toward Luca. "This is his Royal Highness, Prince Luca of Dacia." She met Luca's gaze. "And this is Lady Evelina Davenport."

Luca was too well groomed to not be a

gentleman. He bowed on cue. "It's a pleasure to make your acquaintance."

Lady Evelina's cheeks turned a bright pink. Lenora should feel horrible, but it would do the young lady some good to have the attention of someone as polished as Luca. She curtsied. "The pleasure is all mine, Your Highness."

Luca bowed. "Would you do me the pleasure of joining me for the next set?"

"You want to dance with me?" She pointed at herself and then glanced at Lenora. "But…"

"Enjoy yourself," she told the young girl. "Dancing is the most wonderful feeling in the world." She turned to Luca. "I'm going to the lady's retiring room for a little bit. I'll find you later."

He smiled. "You don't fool me little bird." He leaned a little closer and whispered. "You're going to search for your duke. Happy hunting."

She shook her head and ignored Luca's remark. Julian wasn't at the ball to find. He was right on one hand though. She had no intention of finding the lady's retiring room. There was nothing there she'd like. Most of the ladies would be gossiping and a good number might even be talking about her or Luca. They'd make assumptions as to their connection and make snide comments out of jealousy. All the unattached ladies wanted to be a princess and the already married ones were green with jealousy at the lost opportunity.

Either way Lenora wanted no part of it. So instead she found the exit to the balcony and then took the stairs down to the garden. It would at least be peaceful there and she could find a quiet place to reflect on her feelings for Julian.

JULIAN HADN'T COME IN TO THE BALL BY NORMAL means. He hadn't wanted to go through the long procession line and be formally announced. He had wanted to watch Lady Lenora without her realizing he was in attendance. She didn't appear to be too happy. Her smiles were less frequent and he hadn't seen her dance once. Why was she so miserable? What had happened to make her so unhappy?

When she'd led her prince to the corner and introduced her to Lady Evelina it had shocked him to the core. In that moment he recalled another night when she'd been in that very corner. He'd asked her to dance. It had been a waltz and she'd seemed so happy then. Her smile had been bright and she'd had stars in her eyes. As that memory had rolled over him he had to wonder how he could have failed to recognize her. She'd always been beautiful. It was her shyness that made people overlook her.

Julian had been a complete ass that night. While he'd danced with her he'd realized she could come to mean something to him. So instead of pursuing that connection he'd pushed her away. He recalled making a comment to Holton about having done her a favor by deigning to waltz with her. He'd brushed away those feelings and moved on with his life. At the time he'd had no inclination of settling down with a young beauty. Her innocence shouldn't be tarnished by his roguish ways. Lady Lenora deserved better than him. He'd known it then as sure as he knew it now. The difference was he couldn't walk away this time. He needed her as sure as he needed air to breathe.

The prince was leading Lady Evelina out to the dance floor. She had the same expression of adoration on her face that Lady Lenora had for him a couple years ago. God. He'd messed up. He should never have done his best to push her away then. Julian would have to spend the rest of his days making it up to her. That is if he could convince her to give him a second chance. He wouldn't blame her if she didn't.

She exited the ballroom out on to the balcony. That was his chance to catch her alone. If he had any luck at all she'd go down to the garden. It would give them a measure of privacy that he desperately needed. He stalked toward the balcony and was fast on her heels. She took the steps down to the garden as he'd hoped and entered the maze. His lips twitched. It wasn't a complicated maze but it made a perfect location for a lover's tryst.

He stayed a good distance behind her. Julian wanted her to reach the center of the maze before he made his presence known. She stepped into the heart of the maze. In the middle was an elaborate fountain carved out of marble. It was of the goddess of love, Aphrodite. Julian found it rather appropriate.

She sat down on the bench near the fountain and leaned over to trail her fingers across the water. He stepped forward and admired her beauty in the moonlight. "Beautiful night isn't it?" That was such a stupid thing to say but he didn't know how to even begin a conversation with her. He was an idiot around her these days.

Her head snapped up and she met his gaze.

Lenora's lips twitched as she fought a smile. Julian took that as a good sign. She must be happy to see him. "It's pleasant enough."

"Why are you out here alone?" He moved closer to her keeping his steps languid and easy. "Shouldn't you be inside dancing?"

She shrugged. "I don't feel much like being crushed by all the people Lady Silverly invited."

"It is the largest crowd yet," he agreed. "But that's always a factor in her balls isn't it." He took another step forward. "But you enjoy dancing if I recall. Why not have your prince twirl you around the floor." Why had she led him to Lady Evelina instead? Had she hoped to dance with him and not the prince? Was he seeing things that weren't actually true?

"Luca has all the dancing partners he needs," she said cryptically. "He doesn't need to add me to his dance card."

Julian chuckled. "I didn't realize gentleman started carrying dance cards. I really have been away from social functions too much of late."

"That's not what I meant and you know it." She stood and started to brush past him.

He reached out and stopped her, then leaned down and whispered, "Don't go."

Lenora glanced up and met his gaze. There was uncertainty in her eyes. The same uncertainty that probably mirrored his own eyes. "Why should I stay?"

"Because," he said softly. "If you leave we'll never know for sure."

She licked her lips. "I'm not certain I know what you're talking about."

He leaned down. They were so close their noses were almost touching. All he had to do was move a little bit more and he could press his lips to hers. He wanted to kiss her badly but refrained. Instead he moved a little to the left and kept his mouth close to her ear. "What its like to dance in the moonlight of course."

Her body shook with laughter. "I don't need to dance. Truly."

"What if I do?" He pulled her into his arms. "It's been years since I waltzed with you and I'm craving that particular pleasure. Please Lady Lenora may I have this dance?"

She nibbled adorably on her bottom lip. "I…" Lenora shook her head lightly. "Yes."

He swung her expertly around the center of the garden. Julian twirled her and led them in a circle around Aphrodite under the night sky. It was magical. When he was done they were both breathless and his heart pumped heavily in his chest. With the moonlight glowing overhead he leaned down and pressed his lips to hers as he'd been craving for days.

It was as magical as he imagined it would be. Sparks shot through his whole body. Her lips were sugary like honey and vanilla. Her sweetness was addicting and set him aflame. The kiss shook him to his very soul and in that moment he knew there was no turning back for him. She was the only woman he'd ever want and he intended to make her his forever. All he had to do was convince her that being his wife was the best thing for the both of them. He had a feeling it would take a lot of effort on his part to convince her of his sincerity, but he was willing to kiss her as often as it took to make her accept their fates were intertwined.

CHAPTER 7

*L*enora had wanted to see Julian. Had craved it. When she'd left the ballroom for a stroll in the garden she hadn't believed for a second he might follow her. How could she have? Until the moment he'd stepped out of the shadows she hadn't known he was even in attendance. She'd listened to every announcement and not once had the Duke of Ashley's name been called out by one of the Silverly's servants.

Now he was kissing her. His lips rolled over hers enticingly and coaxed her until she opened them. When he pushed his tongue inside her mouth it had shocked her, but the sensation had amazed her. She touched her tongue to his and then he deepened the kiss. Their tongues dancing together until she moaned from the pleasure of it. It was so decadent and sensual. Never would she have imagined a kiss could be so thrilling. Of course she'd never been kissed before this so how would she have discerned the truth of what it might be like.

Julian pulled her closer. His heat enveloped her and spread over her entire body. No, that wasn't right either. Their bodies were so close together their individual heat mingled together until she had no idea where he began and she ended. If just a kiss could bring them this close together what would it be like if they made love? She shook that thought away. She was not going to allow their passion to go that far. It would mean marriage for certain and she wasn't at all sure she wanted to tie herself to Julian for the rest of her days.

She stepped away from Julian and took several deep breaths. Her lungs burned and her entire body craved to be held by him again. It took every ounce of her self-control to not rush back into his arms. Lenora glanced up at him and met his gaze. His eyelids were heavy and lazy, but filled with intense heat—desire—for her. He wanted her. *Her.* She still couldn't believe it. After she'd worked so hard to become independent and confident that fact still amazed her. That she would compare her worth to this man's feelings for her.

Lenora took another step back. He moved forward, but she held out her hand indicating he should stop. "Don't," she said. "I can't think when you're that close to me."

"Little one…" His voice went low and husky.

Her gaze snapped to his. He'd use that nickname with her all those years ago. That and… little mouse. "Don't try that charm with me." Her voice had hardened at the reminder of their past. When he'd dismissed her as insignificant.

Julian ignored her rebuke. The blasted man's lips twitched upward into one of his sinful heart shattering smiles. Her knees threatened to buckle under the pressure of that charm of his. "There's something between us," he insisted. "I know you feel it too."

She'd always felt something for him, but that didn't mean she had to admit it. Lenora wasn't sure she'd ever be able to openly say it aloud. She'd always loved him. The problem was she wasn't so sure he felt the same way. He liked the new more sophisticated Lenora. The one that was confident and gorgeous. He wanted that version of her on his arm. He'd willingly make love to her, but the wallflower that still threatened to emerge from within—that lady would always be dismissed by the Duke of Ashley. If he'd wanted the wallflower he'd never have dismissed her years ago. "Perhaps there is something there," she conceded. "But that doesn't mean I have to give into the baser side of my nature. I won't let you seduce me into something I might regret later."

"Oh, darling," he said. That tone… It shot straight down her voice and slipped deep inside until she nearly shivered from the sensation. Why did he have to be so charismatic? He took another step toward her. She retreated, but it didn't do any good. He just kept moving forward. Her back hit a large hedge and she had run out of places to go. She was completely trapped and she didn't know what to do. He smiled down at her and she shivered again. "I can promise you one thing. There will be no regrets between us."

That was where he was wrong. She already had regrets. She smiled up at him but sadness permeated through her. Lenora had so many plans and they were ruined the moment she gave into the feelings in her traitorous heart. "Sometimes you're too sure of yourself," she said. "I'm not one of your conquests." She shook her head and reminded herself why she'd left all those years ago. "You can't keep pursuing me as if I asked you to. I won't ever forget that you considered me a little mouse that was insignificant."

He frowned. "You were never unimportant to me."

Her memory of that night a couple years ago came flooding back. *"I can coax any woman to do, well, anything,"* he'd boasted. *"But a wallflower? That's not even a challenge."* He hadn't cared about her then and he didn't now. She lifted her chin and shot those words back at him. "I'm not the wallflower I used to be." Lenora kept her head held high. "All I am to you now is a challenge. I won't give you the satisfaction of taming me. I deserve better than what you have to offer."

He chuckled lightly. "I think the play we saw the other night might be going to your head sweetheart. You're not Kate and I'm not trying to tame you."

The Bard's play, *The Taming of the Shrew*, is what he was comparing her to. It had been what they'd watched in the theater, though she hadn't paid much attention to it at the time.

Lenora wasn't going to stand there and let him insult her. "I never said I was."

He tilted his head to the side. "Perhaps I do see

a little of her in you." Julian frowned. "You're acting like a veritable harpy right now." He sighed. "But I don't want to change you. I would never do that."

Kate hadn't felt as if she belonged. That in her society she was out of place, a stranger—that was why she'd lashed out and used her barbed tongue. It had been her way of defending and protecting herself. Lenora didn't see any problem with that. "That may be," she told him. "But you are trying all the same."

"You're wrong," he disagreed. "But I don't know how to prove myself to you."

She didn't want him to. What would be the point of him going through those motions? She would always find fault with whatever he did. Lenora couldn't trust him. "You don't have to do anything." She really wished he wouldn't bother. Perhaps it was time for her to leave London again.

"Somehow I doubt that, little one."

She gritted her teeth together. "Stop saying that."

"What?" He lifted a brow. Confusion filled his eyes as he met her gaze.

She took a deep breath and said. "I'm not your

little one and I find it condescending that you keep referring to me that way."

He frowned. "I…" Julian shook his head. "I'm sorry. I didn't mean to offend you."

Lenora sighed. "I need to go."

She rushed past him and nearly ran all the way back to the ball. It was definitely time to leave London. If she stayed she would throw herself at Julian. She couldn't allow herself to fall into his arms again. It would only end in disaster.

WHAT THE BLOODY HELL HAD JUST HAPPENED? When he had followed her out to the garden he'd thought that they finally had a chance. That if he only had a few moments alone with her she'd realize they had something real. How could he have messed up so badly? He couldn't even figure out where it had all gone wrong.

He needed a drink. No he needed a whole bottle of brandy. Julian wanted to drown his sorrows and forget about everything. He could go to his club and spend the rest of the evening there. There was no reason for him to remain at the

Silverly ball. Lenora had made her wishes clear. She wanted absolutely nothing to do with him.

At least at his club he would find someone willing to help him forget about her. He could find a game and the patrons at White's would keep the brandy flowing. If that didn't work he could visit Covent Gardens and find a Cyprian. Maybe another woman could help erase the memory of kissing Lenora. Though Julian doubted that was possible. He wanted her. She made his heart beat heavy in his chest. No matter how hard he tried he couldn't stop thinking about her. He'd never been entranced by a woman in his entire life. Lenora was different. He felt something real for her. If only she had felt the same way…

He shook away those thoughts and found the motivation to leave the garden. His heart had shattered but somehow he was still living, breathing… He walked aimlessly until he located his carriage. Julian hopped inside and yelled to the drive, "Take me to White's"

The driver maneuvered the carriage away from the Silverly's and they headed toward the club. Julian crashed back into the velvety softness of the carriage and closed his eyes. He didn't cry, but he felt as if he could. Men didn't cry and he'd be damned if he gave into the urge now. The motion of the carriage lulled him into a sense of oblivion. Several moments past, he couldn't be certain how many, but enough that when the carriage stopped it surprised him. He pushed the curtains to the side and glanced out. They were outside White's.

His heart wasn't in it, but then he was completely numb to anything. He stepped out of the carriage and headed into the club. Once inside he went straight to the card room. The club was bustling with activity, but he hadn't really expected to see any of his friends there. It surprised him to find not only the Marquess of Holton there, but also the Earl of Northesk and the Duke of Clare. He was only mildly acquainted with Clare, but Northesk and Holton were his two closest friends.

Julian wandered over to the table and plopped down in an empty chair. The three of them glanced up at his arrival and grinned. "Ashley," they greeted him in unison. "We were contemplating a game."

"They are still trying to make a decent whist player out of me," Clare said. "I keep trying to tell them I'm not very good at gambling."

"No," Julian agreed. "You don't have the right face for it. Too readable…"

Clare sighed. "That's what Lulia says. She won't

allow me to step foot in their gaming hell. Not that I'd be allowed anyway…all female gaming hell and all that."

Julian lifted a brow. "Whatever are you talking about?"

Northesk shook his head. "That's supposed to be a secret, Clare."

"Right… I forgot." He met Julian's gaze. "Forget I mentioned anything."

He hadn't heard of a female only gaming hell. Julian had thought he knew about everything. He wanted to know more. "I'm afraid it's not that simple," he explained. "You already let to much out of the bag Clare. Tell me all of it."

Holton sighed. "Our wives help run it," he began. "But it's owned by the Duchess of Blackmore. Lady Fortuna's. Even my cousin goes there upon occasion." He met Clare's gaze and pointed a finger at him. "But I blame his wife for that one."

"Lulia and Lenora are fast friends," Clare said and grinned. "She was a quiet thing when she visited us a couple years ago. I barely recognize her now."

Julian frowned. He was fascinated by the idea of an all female gaming hell. How many of the ton's ladies went there to gamble. He wanted to visit it and examine it all for himself—and to top it all off a duchess ran the club. It was almost enough to make him forget about the problems he was having with Lenora. Perhaps he could go to the club and find her there. If he caught her doing something scandalous he might be able to trap her into marriage. It worked for marriage minded ladies. Why couldn't it work for him as well? "Where is this club?"

"No can do," Northesk said. "The only way you're getting that information is if you marry into the circle."

"That's not fair," Julian said. "There has to be another way."

"Well," Holton began. "You could sweet talk one of the ladies into allowing you inside, but that's unlikely as well."

Julian glared at him. "Or one of you could just give me the information."

"No," the all said in unison.

"We all rather like sharing a bed with our wives," Northesk explained. "Nothing you say can convince us to help you out. Sorry."

Well it had been worth a try. "Well perhaps you can assist me with another matter." He motioned for a waiter to come by. When he reached him he said. "Bring a bottle of brandy and a glass for all of us."

The waiter nodded and rushed off to fulfill his request.

"What could you possibly need our help with?" Clare lifted a brow.

"Tell me how you convinced your wives to marry you."

The roars of laughter from all three men echoed around him. Julian had a feeling it was going to be a long night. He shouldn't be surprised, but he was. The waiter brought the bottle of brandy. Once they each had a glass in hand and the brandy was flowing freely they each told their tale. At the end, and after several bottles of brandy, Julian had an idea on how to win Lenora's love. He needed her as much as he needed air to breathe. He refused to give up on her. He loved her too much not to try again and again until he convinced her they belonged together.

CHAPTER 8

*L*enora paced the sitting room uncertain what to do. Julian had kissed her. Made her feel things she thought long buried. How was she to move forward when she nearly shook with emotions she could no longer control. She loved Julian. Had always loved him, and yet, she couldn't trust that he could love her in return. There was so much between them that left her uncertain of him and what he may or may not feel for her. If she couldn't have faith in him how could they possibly have a future together?

They couldn't.

That was the only thing left for her to accept. She would have to leave England again. As long as she was close to Julian she'd never be able to have any sort of life. She would constantly be plagued with doubts and that was no way to live.

"What has you so broody?"

Lenora glanced up and met her friend, Lulia's gaze. Should she tell her the truth or deflect it as nothing? After a moments consideration she decided on the truth. Lulia had always been able to see through her and go straight to the heart of the matter. It wouldn't do her any good to pretend that she was all right when that couldn't be farther from the truth. "Julian kissed me."

"Did he?" Lulia lifted a brow. "Then why, pray tell, are you miserable? Isn't this what you wanted?" Her gypsy accent was thick as she spoke.

"I…" Had this been what she'd hoped for? Julian noticed her and that had been her main goal. But what had she expected to gain from it? "I'm confused," she admitted.

"That much is clear." Lulia stepped closer to her. "I must confess this does not surprise me. You had a vengeful heart when you visited me in Tenby."

"Then why did you agree to assist me?"

Lulia smiled warmly at her. "Because I have a soft spot for lost souls in need of rescuing." She moved over to the settee and sat. "Come here and rest a moment. How long have you been pacing this room?"

"I'm not sure…a while."

"Much longer and you're going to wear the carpet down to nothing." Lulia chuckled softly.

Lenora sighed and then did as Lulia had suggested. She went to a chair and plopped down. She couldn't recall the last time she'd been so miserable. No, that wasn't true. She'd felt this way when she'd overheard Julian dismissing her as nothing after their first dance together. This time was different though. She'd been the one to walk away from him. "What do I do?"

"That is for you to decide," Lulia told her. "You went away and I encouraged it, but not for the reasons you believe."

Lenora tilted her head to the side. "You don't think I had a noble enough reason?"

"Revenge is never a good reason for anything. It only leads to heartbreak." Her tone was firm and understanding at the same time. "You needed the time away to discover who you were. Did I like the reason you wanted to do all of that? No." She shook her head. "But I did understand it. What you need to do now is decide what it is you really want. Is revenge enough or are you brave enough to love him and accept him faults and all." She met Lenora's gaze. "Can you take a chance on love and the prospect of a lifetime of happiness?"

Lenora froze at her words. "What if he hasn't told me he loves me?"

She lifted a brow. "Have you spoken the word to him?"

"No," she admitted. Saying them made it all real and she hadn't been ready to do that. "I'm afraid."

"We all are," Lulia admitted. "When you lay your emotions bare before someone you leave yourself open to a world of hurt. But you also open yourself up to the possibilities." She leaned over and patted Lulia's hand. "No one is perfect, Nora. If that were the case how boring would the world be? Our differences are what makes everything interesting." Her lips tilted upward into a serene smile. "Your Julian made a mistake. Do you believe he must pay for that error in judgment forever or do you want to forgive him for his arrogant male ego and allow him to make it right."

When she put it that way it made Lenora feel like all kinds of wrong. She'd been looking at Julian through visions of her past with him. She'd changed in the past couple of years so it was possible he had as well. He had seemed different with her. Less…pompous or arrogant and more open. "I want him." She always had. "I'm just not sure how to…"

"Tell him that?" Lulia finished for her. "That is the hard part and where you will have to take a leap of faith. I'll leave that to you to unravel. Something tells me that you'll cross paths again soon and when you do don't lose courage. The only way you're going to find your happiness is to admit how you feel. After that the rest won't seem quite as difficult." Lulia stood and smiled down at her. "I must be off now. Come visit me afterward. You will be in my thoughts." With those words she left Lenora alone with a lot to think of.

She had to find Julian, but she didn't know where to even begin. Lenora sighed. Maybe she should just wait until the ball later that night. Perhaps he'd attend again and she could steal a moment alone with him. It was the best she could hope for until she next was in his presence…

JULIAN HAD MADE A LOT OF PLANS AFTER HE'D LEFT his club. He'd thought back to that night he'd danced with Lenora. The one where he'd first called her little one. He'd also called her little mouse… It had seemed fitting at the time, but she was no meek miss anymore. She may have been timid then, but she was a vibrant, strong-willed, woman now. One that could match him in every way… He loved her and wanted to spend the rest of his life with her at his side. She'd make a perfect duchess. He just had to convince her to take a chance on loving him.

He'd gone home and found his mother's ring. The ring was gold with a square cut ruby and tiny diamonds flanking it. It was a family heirloom that had been worn by every Duchess of Ashley. He intended for Lenora to wear it as well. He would not relent until she agreed to marry him. Even if it took years he would not give up on her.

He patted his coat to ensure the ring was still in his inside pocket then walked into the Bristol ball. Lady Bristol's goal each season was to outdo the Silverly ball. She never quite managed to meet the attendance as Lady Silverly, but she could be counted on for lavish entertainments and decadent surroundings. Julian really didn't care either way. He wasn't there for the ball. There was only one reason for him to have accepted the invitation—

Lenora. He hoped she would be there and he could have at the very least a dance with her.

Music echoed throughout the ball. He'd slipped in through the back entrance again. Julian had always hated formality and didn't like being announced. He hated being stared at and fawned over. It was much more to his liking to pay a servant to give him access to the event by other means. Julian stood on the edges of the ballroom searching for Lenora.

Lady Bristol had been successful in luring many of the ton's elite to her ball. The ballroom was nearly bursting at the seams. It was hard to see anyone amongst the crush of people in the room. He was about to give up when he caught a glimpse of something out of the corner of his eye. He turned as Lenora was exiting the ballroom. He grinned. She had a penchant for gardens and balconies. Not that he blamed her… He hated the stuffiness of an overcrowded ballroom too.

He brushed past several people rushing toward the exit she'd taken. It took him longer than he wanted to reach the fine glass doors. He slid outside and breathed in the fresh night air. The moonlight glowed over the stone balcony. Lenora stood at the edge with her head tipped upward as if she was basking in the moon's light. Julian stepped forward mesmerized by her beauty.

"Lenora," he said. Her name was huskier than he intended. His emotions were running rampant through him. Julian couldn't remember ever being as nervous as he was in that moment.

She turned toward him. Her dark hair shimmered in the light and she looked like an ethereal princess. A goddess come to life and deigning to acknowledge his presence… He stepped closer like a being tempted by the radiance of the sun—too foolish to realize that if it got too close it could be burned alive. To have her he'd risk anything.

"Yes?" She lifted a brow. Her lips twitched a little but he wasn't certain if it was amusement or anger. Her face was completely unreadable.

He continued to move toward her. "Will you…" Julian swallowed hard not able to grasp the necessary words to reach her.

"Will I what?" she asked. Lenora stayed leaning against the balcony, unyielding.

"I'd like to dance with you," he finally said. It seemed like a safe topic to broach with her.

"Just a dance?" She lifted a brow. "There's nothing else you want from me?" There was a hitch in her tone he didn't recognize. Was she as uncertain as he was? Did he dare ask for more than that? Would she accept him?

He took another step forward until he was close enough to reach out and touch her. Julian wanted to kiss her again, but he didn't risk it, at least not yet. "There is much I'd ask of you," he began. "But I don't wish to push you away with my yearnings. If it is your desire to take things…slow." He swallowed hard and then took a deep breath to muster the courage to keep speaking. "I'm willing to follow your lead."

"Why?" She asked softly. "What is it about me you find so appealing?"

"Everything," he said. "I know you might not believe that, but there's nothing about you I don't adore. I love you and if you'll allow me to I'll cherish you for the rest of my days…" He lifted his hand to caress her cheek. "I understand if you don't believe me. There have been times I've been a complete arse." A tear slipped from her eye and trailed down her cheek. He wiped it away with the pad of his thumb. "Don't cry sweetheart. It kills me to see you hurting."

She lifted her lips into a wobbly smile. "They're happy tears…" She stepped into his arms and rested her head on his chest. "I should be apologizing to you. I've been so judgmental…"

"You had every right to be," he told her. "I haven't always been someone you could rely on." He hadn't really believed she'd be even this accepting. The moonlight must be working some kind of magic for him. Should he push his luck and ask for her hand?

"I've had to do a lot of soul searching myself." She met his gaze. "And someone pointed out to me today that not everyone is perfect. We all make mistakes and I've made plenty." She leaned up and pressed her lips to his in a brief kiss. "What I'm trying to say is I'm going to try to not be so difficult, but I might not be able to help myself from time to time." She licked her lips. "I love you. I've always loved you."

His heart thundered inside his chest. "Good," he breathed out the word. "Because I can't imagine my life without you. Please marry me." He stepped back long enough to pull out the ring from his pocket. "Say yes, little one." He groaned. The nickname slipped out and he couldn't take it back. Julian prayed it wouldn't make her say no or run from him again.

She smiled. "It's all right," she told him. "It's an

endearment and I've actually started to like it a little bit." She held out her hand to him. "And yes, I'll marry you."

He breathed a sigh of relief and pushed the ring on to her finger. It was a night he wouldn't ever forget. She'd agreed to be his duchess and give him the chance to love her properly for the rest of his days. There wasn't anything he could ever want more. Julian leaned down and kissed her the way he'd been wanting to since he walked out on to the balcony. He couldn't wait to marry her so he could make love to her. For now though, it was enough to have the right to kiss her. She was his and always would be…

EPILOGUE

Lenora stood at the entrance of Fortuna's Parlor. It had been a while since she'd gone into the women's gaming hell. She'd never been much of a gambler and had only gone to visit Lulia. The duchess taught fencing to ladies who wished to learn, and some of them even sparred in real matches that bets could be placed. Lady Diana, the countess of Northesk, handled that aspect of the gaming hell. Lady Katherine, the Marchioness of Holton, her cousin's wife bred horses for the horseracing portion. The owner, the Duchess of Blackmore, liked horses and ensured she always had a horse in the race. She'd even purchased some of Lady Katherine's horses hoping to build on her already expanding stock.

But none of that mattered because she wasn't there for any sort of gambling. It was Christmastide and they were all gathering at Fortuna's to celebrate together. Sure there would be some sort of gambling and entertainments, but that wasn't the main purpose. This event was to bring everyone together and enjoy the holiday season. Everyone had found love and they wanted to rejoice in that.

Well everyone except Luca…

He had stayed in London and Lenora hoped he would find someone to love as much as she loved Julian. She was so happy she wanted all of her friends to be as content as she was. Luca seemed to be more and more miserable every day.

She walked into the gaming hell located above a seamstress shop. Normally only ladies were allowed inside, but since it was a special occasion the husbands and some of their male friends were allowed in. Luca was one of those male friends. He stood in a corner glaring at someone across the room. She followed his line of sight and discovered the subject of his ire. Lady Evelina Davenport stood near the entrance to the fencing room speaking to Lulia. She must want to learn how to fence. That was an interesting development.

Was Luca interested in Lady Evelina? She was a

lovely girl and she'd make a wonderful princess. That was if she wanted to marry Luca and move to the tiny island nation of Dacia... Lenora would have to take the time to speak to the girl. If Luca was interested in Lady Evelina she wanted to encourage the connection.

"What has you smiling?" Julian stood behind her and had leaned down to whisper in her ear. His hot breath sent shivers down her spine. She loved him so darn much...

"It appears Lulia is taking another little mouse under her wing," she nodded toward the duchess and Lady Evelina.

"I'd be terrified," he began. "If I wasn't already madly in love with you." He grinned wickedly. "Who do you think she's grooming her for?"

"Does it matter?" She returned his smile with a wanton one of her own. "It will lead to someone else's happy-ever-after. I'm on board for that sort of outcome."

"When you put it that way," he said before he leaned down and pressed his lips to hers. "It doesn't sound so bad. I'm inclined to agree considering how much I adore you. If not for Lulia's meddling we might not have found our way to each other."

"Perhaps," she said. "I'm not so sure. Sometimes fate has a way of working out the way it's supposed to. I believe Lulia just pushed us in the right direction a little sooner than we might have otherwise gone."

"Either way it's perfect for me." He pulled her closer. "After all marrying you was the best thing that I've ever done." He nodded at Lulia and Evelina. "I have no doubt that whoever that lady chooses will be the best person for her too. I'm hopeful where I never was before."

"That's good. I have a gift for you. Do you want it now or later?"

"I'm guessing it's nothing too wicked or you wouldn't offer it to me now," he said and then grinned. "So I'm willing to take what you're offering and take what I really want later."

She stepped on to her tiptoes and whispered in his ear, "I'm pregnant."

The sounds of his happiness echoed through the room. Everyone stopped and stared briefly, but then turned back to their conversation. Happiness could be contagious and she suspected most of the people at Fortuna's had their own version to keep them warm at night. She was just glad to have her own slice of it and Julian to love forever. Taking a chance on love was the best decision she'd ever made and soon they'd have a child to share that love with. She couldn't possibly ask for anything more…

AFTERWORD

Thank you so much for taking the time to read my book.
Your opinion matters!
Please take a moment to review this book on your favorite review site and share your opinion with fellow readers.

www.authordawnbrower.com

ABOUT THE AUTHOR

USA TODAY Bestselling author, DAWN BROWER writes both historical and contemporary romance. There are always stories inside her head; she just never thought she could make them come to life. That creativity has finally found an outlet.

Growing up she was the only girl out of six children. She is a single mother of two teenage boys; there is never a dull moment in her life. Reading books is her favorite hobby and she loves all genres.

- bookbub.com/authors/dawn-brower
- facebook.com/1DawnBrower
- twitter.com/1DawnBrower
- instagram.com/1DawnBrower

ALSO BY DAWN BROWER

Broken Pearl

Deadly Benevolence

A Wallflower's Christmas Kiss

A Gypsy's Christmas Kiss

Snowflake Kisses

Begin Again

There You'll Be

Better as a Memory

Won't Let Go

Enduring Legacy

The Legacy's Origin

Charming Her Rogue

Scandal Meets Love

Love Only Me (Amanda Mariel)

Find Me Love (Dawn Brower)

If It's Love (Amanda Mariel)

Odds of Love (Dawn Brower)

Coming Soon

Believe In Love (Amanda Mariel)

Chance of Love (Dawn Brower)

Christmas at Fortuna's Parlor (Amanda Mariel and Dawn Brower)

Bluestockings Defying Rogues

When An Earl Turns Wicked

A Lady Hoyden's Secret

One Wicked Kiss

Earl In Trouble

All the Ladies Love Coventry

Coming Soon

One Less Scandalous Earl

Confessions of a Hellion

Marsden Descendants

Rebellious Angel

Tempting An American Princess

Coming Soon

How to Kiss a Debutante

Loving an America Spy

Marsden Romances

A Flawed Jewel

A Crystal Angel

A Treasured Lily

A Sanguine Gem

A Hidden Ruby

A Discarded Pearl

Novak Springs

Cowgirl Fever

Dirty Proof

Unbridled Pursuit

Sensual Games

Christmas Temptation

Linked Across Time

Saved by My Blackguard

Searching for My Rogue

Seduction of My Rake

Surrendering to My Spy

Spellbound by My Charmer

Stolen by My Knave

Separated from My Love

Scheming with My Duke

Secluded with My Hellion

Heart's Intent

One Heart to Give

Unveiled Hearts

Heart of the Moment

Kiss My Heart Goodbye

Heart in Waiting

Broken Curses

The Enchanted Princess

The Bespelled Knight

The Magical Hunt

Ever Beloved

Forever My Earl

Always My Viscount

Infinitely My Marquess

EternallyMyDuke

Kismet Bay

Once Upon a Christmas

New Year Revelation

All Things Valentine

Luck At First Sight

Endless Summer Days

Coming Soon

A Witch's Charm

All Out of Gratitude

Christmas Ever After

Love Only Me

Scandal Meets Love

USA TODAY BESTSELLING AUTHOR
Amanda Mariel

CHAPTER 1

Suffolk, England
April 1812

Lady Narissa Goodwin had never been the conventional sort. Raised by her gambler father, she'd grown up around card games, horse races, and drinking. As she strolled across the turf at Newmarket, ready to ride her horse Merlin, she glanced at the crowd of spectators gathered for the race. Narissa could not be more ready for the days' events. A grin spread across her face.

Gentlemen lined the course dressed in fine day coats and breeches, their cravats starched and tied expertly. Bookmakers collected wagers and called out odds while jockeys mounted their horses and prepared for the race. The thrill of the day vibrated in the air. A slight spring breeze cooled her skin and the sun shone brightly. There could not be a more perfect day for a race.

Her gaze stopped on a group of ladies who peered at her with disapproval radiating from their eyes. Narissa paid them no mind as she turned her attention back to the turf. Before long, she would be racing along the course, Merlin's hoofs pounding beneath her. A controlled wildness one would have to experience to understand, and she thrived on it. She cared not what a group of dull ladies thought about her.

Papa's words echoed in her head, 'You have but one life. Live it on your own terms, Poppet'. Narissa did just that, she raced with the best, ran her own gaming hell, and lived by her own set of rules—society be damned. She notched her chin confidently as she took Merlin's reins.

"Thank you," she said to the groom.

He offered a smile and nod before she glanced back at the crush of people assembled beyond the track. A few ladies standing closer to the turf than ladies normally did had been watching her but turned away when she caught their gaze. She recognized one of them, Lady Ophelia, wife of an earl. The lady frequented Narissa's gaming hell, Fortuna's Parlor, named after her first thoroughbred. A gift from her beloved papa for her thirteenth birthday.

At the club, Lady Ophelia went out of her way to chat with Narissa. Funny how differently the lady treated her in public, but then, many of her patrons acted in the same manner, save for a few close friends.

Most of the *ton's* ladies kept their parlor doors closed to Narissa and shunned her on the streets, but the gentlemen did not share their sentiments. Rarely did a man shoot her a disapproving glare or speak out against her. In fact, they tended to act as if she belonged among them, allowing her to join their card games and such. Perhaps it was a result of having known her papa. Perhaps it was the source of the ladies scorn for her? Regardless, she did not give a whit.

She nudged the chestnut colt into motion. Narissa had been anticipating this race for months. Excitement thrummed in her veins as the well-muscled horse moved beneath her. She'd been born for this. Leastwise that is what Papa had always said, and she most certainly believed it.

The thrill of racing was in her blood the same

as it was Merlin's. Together, they were a force the likes of which the *ton* had not seen before. All of England would soon know it. Merlin ran fast and free like the wind, a born racer. Her own spirited nature only served to compliment the thoroughbreds. Together they were unstoppable. Drawing him to a halt at the starting line, she stroked the animals' neck. "Let us show them what we are made of," she whispered.

Papa crossed her mind and she glanced up at the heavens. She'd give anything for him to be here now. He would be exceedingly pleased. Merlin had been bred from Papa's prize stallion, and it had been his dream to race the horse. Together they had started the horses' training. After Papa passed away, she was determined to see his dream brought to reality.

She closed her eyes. *Papa, I hope you are watching.* A gentle breeze wrapped around her as if in answer and her chest tightened. She missed him dearly—always would. In her heart, she knew he was watching, cheering, as he would at Epsom, and she found a measure of comfort in the knowledge. Papa had always been her champion.

She turned her attention to the other riders lining up for the Two Thousand Guineas sweepstakes race over the Riley Mile. The twelve-horse field looked impressive, though it did not shake her confidence in Merlin. He could outrun all of them. The bookkeepers had picked him as the favorite. She'd heard the frenzy of betting with many gentlemen placing wagers on her mount. She, too, had bet on Merlin for the win.

Even now, a crowd surrounded the bookmaker, placing last-minute wagers. Off to the side, a tall man with midnight black hair caught her attention. The way he studied her with his piercing blue eyes sent a chill straight through her. Who the deuce was he? And why did he take such an interest in her?

Narissa tore her gaze away, determined not to let the stranger shake her. She bent low over Merlin, then inhaled his scent, calming herself. Nature, the mingling of hay, horse sweat, and dust—there was nothing more refreshing, more capable of bringing her into the moment.

Merlin bolted at the signal to start. Narissa's muscles strained with the effort required to hold him back. Heart pounding, excitement thrumming through her, she focused on the course awaiting the perfect time to loosen her hold on the reins, and unleash Merlin's full speed. Yes, this is what she lived for—the thrill of competition. The satisfaction found in victory. And make no mistake, victory would be hers.

∞

Seth Blakey, Duke of Blackmore, could not take his attention from the turf. Not that he wished to as his own horse, Highflier, was among the racers. However, it was the lady rider that held him captive. Where had she come from? And what the devil was a female doing jockeying at Newmarket? This was a competitive male field, not suitable for the gentler sex.

Prying his attention from her, he looked at the whole field of horses. Highflier had the lead by a head. His competition, a well-muscled black, fought to close the gap, while the rest of the horses ran in a cluster a few furlongs behind. The woman trailed the field at the back of the pack, though not by any great distance.

Calls of 'Come on', 'Go, Merlin, go', 'Come on Highflier', and 'Move Gypsy Dancer, filled the air around him. A frenzy of chants and curses from the crowd rang out from the sidelines as the horses approached the final stretch.

Seth remand silent, his focus on the woman

whose mount was overtaking the field with a burst of speed. Merlin took to the inside, passing the cluster of trailing horses before closing the distance on Highflier and the black who remained neck in neck with him. Bloody hell, the woman could ride. And she'd not used the whip at all.

For the first time since the race began, he saw the real possibility of losing. Something he could not abide. He leaned closer to the rail and bellowed, "Move it, Highflier. Use the damn whip!" His gaze skittered between the three horses battling it out for the lead.

"Come on Highflier!" he yelled as his horse and Merlin pulled ahead of the black, nose and nose. Not only did he stand to lose the prize purse, but he'd also bet ten thousand pounds on Highflier winning. "Use the whip, dammit!" He screamed across the turf at his own jockey as Merlin pulled into the lead. What the devil was his rider doing?

Pulse thrumming, he tossed his program to the ground as Merlin raced across the finish line leaving Highflier in second place. Merlin and his female rider were not among the initial field of entrants, but were late editions added only this morning. A complete surprise that left him at a disadvantage, not that he would have scratched

Highflier from the race—he could not have even if he'd wanted to.

Bloody hell, he should have won. Who the hell was the woman? And where had that horse come from? Determined to find out, Seth moved toward the finish line.

"Your Grace," a baritone voice called after him.

His irritation increased as he turned toward the man. "Lord Stanford." The older man smiled, his brown eyes sparkling, the skin at their edges creased with age.

"Your horse ran a fine race, today. If not for Merlin, you surely would have won."

Seth swallowed. He did not need nor want a reminder of what had just occurred. Though he did have unanswered questions. "Who is the woman that rode Merlin?"

Lord Stanford glanced to where the jockeys now congregated. "A true hoyden that one. Lady Narissa Goodwin. She's a rare breed, beautiful and brazen. There should be more like her."

Goodwin. Where had Seth heard that name? He looked at the beauty that had dismounted and removed her riding cap, revealing tightly bound chestnut locks. "Lord Haddington's daughter?"

"Indeed." The older man clapped a hand on

Seth's shoulder. "Ladies like her breed excitement. They keep a man young, you know." He flashed a fine set of crafted ivories. "In my day they ruled society."

Seth disagreed with the old man's musings, though he kept his opinion to himself. Women like Lady Narissa were foolish. They would bring a man to ruin and had no care for their own reputations or safety. It mattered not to him, for he had no desire for lasting connections. Though he may have a short-term use for this particular hellion. "If you will excuse me."

Lord Stanford gave a nod before turning away.

Seth strolled through the crush of spectators, toward Lady Narissa. A crowd of gentlemen surrounded her, offering their congratulations and complimenting her skill as well as her mount. He stopped short of reaching her to watch the frenzy and wait for his opening. Squinting against the sun's rays, Seth studied her from the shiny braided mass of hair at the back of her head to her boot-clad feet.

Her golden eyes twinkled against her tanned skin reminding him of fine whisky. Full pink lips grinned at her crowd of admirers, emitting whimsical laughter now and again as the gentleman spoke. She could not be much over five feet tall. An imp of a woman, but Lord Stanford had been correct. Lady Narissa was indeed a beauty. The fact only served to rankle him more.

She said something he could not make out, then began moving away from her admirers. This was his chance. Seth sprinted after her, calling out her name, "Lady Narissa."

"I truly must be—" Her gaze caught on him, brows creasing. "Have we meet?"

"No. I am the Duke of Blackmore, Seth Blakey." He offered a friendly smile, his annoyance at having lost the race forgotten the moment he drew near her.

"A pleasure to meet you, Your Grace." She glanced down, swiping a hand over her dusty riding jacket. "Perhaps we will become better acquainted some other time." She turned to take her leave.

How dare the vixen dismiss him? "Wait," he said in a firm tone he hoped brokered no argument.

Scowling, she returned her attention to him. "I haven't the time for games right now."

"Very well then, I will cut straight to the point." He rocked back on his heels. "I want you to ride Highflier at Epsom."

"I will be riding, Merlin. Good day, Your

Grace." She turned on her heels and began to march away.

"I will give you five thousand pounds," he called after her.

"Keep your blunt." She tossed the words over her shoulder. The sway of her hips confident as she grew smaller in the distance.

Had he ever met a more self-assured, infuriating woman? She acted as if he were below her. A bothersome pest circling her tiara. Yet, he found himself captivated, wanting to know more about her. A foolish notion, he was certain.

Seth kicked at the ground, causing a plume of dust to fill the air. Let the hellion ride Merlin. It would make no difference to him. He'd train more speed into his mount. Find a more skilled rider. Do whatever was necessary to win at Epsom. As it were, his horse had nearly won. If he trained him a bit harder, Highflier could, no would, beat Merlin. In the meantime, he would keep an eye on Tattersall's offerings. The she-devil would not best him at Epsom.

Not unless she changed her mind and rode for him.

CHAPTER 2

London, England

Narissa strolled across Madam Josephine Debroux's shop, a smile curving her lips when she found Josephine relaxing in her office.

"Do tell." Josephine repositioned herself on the gold brocade chair she'd been lounging in. "Did you find victory?"

Narissa took the chair opposite from her modiste, who was in truth, more of a friend. "The competition was stiff, but the odds favored Merlin." She paused, meeting Josephine's warm gaze. "We were victorious indeed."

A wide grin spread across Josephine's face, her

EXCERPT: LOVE ONLY ME

warm gaze sparkling. "I knew you would be. Never doubted it." She beamed. "Your papa would be so proud. Let us celebrate." Josephine strolled from her office to the dress shop door and turned the lock.

Narissa stood, smoothing the wrinkles from her green dress. She had bathed and donned a frock hastily before coming to Madame Debroux's, intent to see her friend and check on her gaming hell. When Josephine returned to the office, Narissa said, "Then let us go above stairs and have a scotch. I dearly wish to check on my club."

Josephine gave a nod, signaling for Narissa to lead the way.

Narissa strolled through the shop to the door hidden behind the fitting room that displayed the name of her secret, all female gaming hell, Fortuna's Parlor. The letters scrolled in black across a brass plate. In the rear of the building, another door led into the club, but it bore no sign in order to maintain secrecy. All the same, her members were familiar with it as well as how to gain entry.

Narissa had made a fortune gambling with her pin money before papa passed away. After his death, she came up with the idea for Fortuna's Parlor. During a fitting for new riding clothes, she shared her desire to open a female gaming club with Josephine—her longtime modest. Josephine offered to rent Narissa the space above her shop, and Fortuna's was born.

Now Narissa did all she could to guard her club and see it flourish. She catered to societies upper crust ladies and their need for both adventure and secrecy. All the while, Narissa watched her fortune grow while doing the things she most enjoyed. She'd managed to carve out her own version of a perfect life.

Narissa pulled open the door and started up the stairs with Josephine behind her. The dark haired man from Newmarket sprang into the forefront of her mind. Why the devil had he upset her so? It wasn't as if he'd been the first man to ever study her. Nor had he been the first to incite her anger. She glanced back at her friend. "There was a man at the race."

"Several, I imagine." Josephine gave a wave of her hand. "What makes one stand out from the rest?"

"I noticed him watching me before the race started. He seemed to be studying me, and I must admit that I found it rather unsettling. It was as if he knew I had secrets and wished to discover them." Narissa glanced around the grand space before she strolled toward her office.

She had a full house tonight. Ladies sat around green baize tables, some chatting and laughing, others with serious expressions focused on the game at hand—faro, whist, *rouge et noir*, and hazard among them. Tonight would be profitable, indeed. She grinned.

Narissa caught Lady Brooke Lynwood's attention and waved her over to join their celebration. Brooke, the daughter of an earl, had been one of Fortuna's first members and had become a close friend to Narissa. She was one of few ladies who did not publicly shun Narissa while embracing her privately. Furthermore, the pair had much in common and lived by similar philosophies —neither giving a fig for what the *ton* deemed appropriate.

Leaving the door ajar for Brooke, Narissa and Josephine entered the office. "It was almost as though he were looking into my soul. He had the most captivating blue eyes." She shuddered at the memory emblazoned into her mind. "I swear they cut right through me."

"Did you speak with him?" Josephine lifted a

decanter from the carved mahogany sideboard and began pouring tumblers of scotch.

"Speak with whom?" Lady Brooke stepped into the office closing the door behind her.

Narissa accepted a tumbler from Josephine and took a drink, relishing the heat that spread through her, before replying. "His Grace, the Duke of Blackmore. And indeed, I did."

"I am acquainted with him." Brooke took the tumbler Josephine offered. "I have played cards with his sister, Lady Hannah, a few times. I met him through her, though it was but a brief introduction. He is a handsome devil."

"Never mind him. I am far more interested in his sister." Narissa strolled to the window that overlooked the gaming floor. Papa would love what she'd created here. An image of him playing at the tables formed in her mind. How many times had she witnessed such a scene growing up?

Her mind flashed back to the first time Papa had allowed her to join in on a game. She'd been sixteen and the only lady in the card room. Papa had beamed and jested good naturally with the other gentleman when Narissa won. From that day forward, she was always allowed a seat at the table when the gentleman gathered. God, she missed him.

Narissa turned back to Brooke. "Is the lady fit for membership?"

"I believe she would be a good addition." Scotch in hand, Brooke positioned herself on a chaise. "She is free-spirited and holds her own around a deck of playing cards."

"Bring her tomorrow night." Narissa stared out at the crush of gambling ladies.

What did she hope to accomplish by meeting the duke's sister? She did not know, however, it could only benefit her to learn more about the man in case they should cross paths again. Papa had long ago taught her to keep as many tricks as possible up her sleeve. Lady Hannah would be an ace against her brother, the Duke of Blackmore, should Narissa ever require one.

"I can do better than tomorrow. I am to meet with her this evening, within the hour as a matter of fact. We were to go for a ride in Hyde Park. I will bring her here instead." Blue eyes sparkling, Brooke lowered her glass to the marble table beside her, "If it pleases you."

"Indeed it does." Narissa sighed, her shoulders relaxing.

"Are you planning to keep us in suspense all night?" Josephine asked from where she leaned against the sideboard. "Or do you intend to tell us about your duke?"

"He is *not* my anything." Narissa took another deep drink. "All the same, I will fill you in."

Josephine settled more comfortably, her attention solidly trained on Narissa.

"After the race, once my well-wishers had dispersed, the duke approached me. He requested that I ride for him at Epsom."

Brooke's eyes rounded. "The nerve! Surely, he knew you rode for yourself."

"I do not know that he did. After all, Merlin is still registered under Papa's name." Narissa ran her finger around the rim of her tumbler. "I really must update that. All the same, I have no wish to ride for anyone else and I told the duke as much."

"Good for you," Josephine said, giving a matter of fact nod of her head.

"Thank you." Narissa smiled, she did so adore these women and considered herself kissed by good fortune that she got to refer to them as friends. "After I declined, the duke offered to pay me an absurd sum to change my mind. Five thousand pounds, can you imagine?"

"I may have agreed for that much blunt." Josephine carried the decanter to Narissa before topping off her tumbler.

"Say you did not." Brooke held her own glass out for a refill. "It is a great deal of coin, but you are already wealthy."

"Of course I stayed steadfast, refusing the offer and marching away." Though a part of her wished she'd entertained the duke a bit more. Allowed the conversation to go further. Not that she ever would have agreed to ride for him.

Josephine raised her tumbler. "Cheers to you, my lady, my friend."

"Cheers, indeed." Brooke followed suit. "As well as congratulations on your most recent win."

Narissa lifted her tumbler. "And here is to victory at Epsom."

The duke would be there, and she would not cede to him. Merlin had better times than any horse she had ever trained. He ran a mile in under two minutes and required no whip. Furthermore, he ran equally well on dirt or grass. She doubted there were many other horses out there like him, and fewer capable of besting him. The duke would soon know it, too.

"Yes, to Epsom." Brooke notched her chin.

"And to besting the duke." Josephine winked. "I'd wager all I have that your father is proud as a peacock watching over you."

Narissa smiled, then drained her glass. She looked at Brooke. "Do bring the duke's sister at once. I should very much like to make her acquaintance."

Brooke nodded, rising from her seat. "I will return within a couple hours' time."

Narissa placed her tumbler on the sideboard. It would not serve her to be foxed when the lady arrived. "Thank you, Brooke."

Josephine retrieved a deck of cards from the top of Narissa's desk as Brooke took her leave. "Shall we pass the time with a friendly game of piquet?"

Narissa accepted the cards and began shuffling as she took a seat near the fireplace.

"While we are at it, you can tell me what you have planned for the duke's sister." Josephine gave a knowing grin.

"How is it that you understand me so well?" Narissa laughed, then without waiting for an answer, said, "I am not certain as of yet, but believe she could prove useful."

"Indeed." Josephine fanned her cards out.

After several hands of piquet, a knock came at

the door, drawing Narissa's attention. It had to be Brooke with the duke's sister. Her excitement spiked. "Enter."

Lady Brooke strolled in, followed by a petite woman with midnight curls and the same piercing blue eyes as the duke. Narissa sat her cards aside and stood. "You must be Lady Hannah."

"And you must be Lady Narissa. Brooke has told me a great deal about you and your club. I am honored to be here." The lady bestowed a genuine smile, excitement radiating from her.

"It is my pleasure to have you. And do call me Narissa. We are all friends here." Narissa retrieved a tumbler and offered it to the lady. "Come, sit."

Hannah accepted, taking a sip of the scotch before positioning herself on the chase near Brooke. "It is very impressive…what you have built here."

"Fortuna's is a labor of love." Narissa offered a grin. "Is it your wish to become a member?"

"I would very much like the honor." Hannah returned Narissa's smile.

"Then let us get to know each other better." Narissa sipped from her scotch. "Tell us all about you. Your family, hobbies, leave nothing out."

Hannah sat her tumbler aside and folded her hands in her lap. "I am afraid there isn't much to tell. My parents are deceased. The duke of Blackmore is my brother and guardian. He brought me to London hoping to secure a suitable marriage for me."

"Do you wish to be married?" Narissa studied her finding nothing off in the tone of her voice or her body language.

"No, leastwise not yet. Once married, I fear that I will lose the freedom to do the things that I enjoy."

"Such as?" Narissa prodded.

Hannah retrieved her tumbler and held it up. "For starters, a husband is not likely to approve of me drinking scotch." She tipped the glass against her lips and drained the contents. "Nor would he approve of my spending time in a gaming hell or attending secret female fencing matches in darkened gardens."

"I take it you have met Lady Diana?"

Hannah smiled. "Indeed. I found her delightful."

Josephine retrieved the decanter and refilled Hannah's tumbler before topping of Narissa and Brooke's. "Do you enjoy fencing?"

"Regrettably, I have never had the occasion to try my hand at the sport. I do rather enjoy spectating though."

Narissa swirled the scotch in her glass. "Does your brother approve of how you spend your time?"

"Heaven's no." Hannah shook her head. "He doesn't know the half of it, but what he does know makes him want to lock me away."

Narissa laughed. She had the distinct feeling that whether or not she learned anything useful about the duke, Hannah would be a welcome addition to the club.

EXCERPT: WHEN AN EARL TURNS WICKED

BLUESTOCKINGS DEFYING ROGUES
BOOK ONE

DAWN BROWER

USA TODAY
BESTSELLING AUTHOR

Dawn Brower

When an Earl Turns Wicked

PROLOGUE

Southington Castle, England, 1808

The day was like any other one in England. Rainfall had become a normal enough occurrence that Jonas didn't notice it—even as it dripped down his face, drenching him completely. He stared at the chiseled stones in the cemetery near Southington's chapel. Only members of his family were buried there—many he never met personally. Pictures of them filled the great hall, but they were history to him, and he'd been able to distance himself from their stories. This, however, was far different.

His life would never be the same. The death of

his father had marked an unchangeable truth. The duke now had control over Jonas's life. His grandfather was a tyrant and had always attempted to browbeat his will into him. His father had been the one person he'd been able to count on. A buffer the duke couldn't break through, and he'd tried often.

So, no, the cold didn't matter because he was numb through and through. Rain? Paltry in comparison to what he had yet to face. The Duke of Southington, his grandfather, hadn't started yet —mainly because he couldn't. There were people around, and he dared not cause a scene. Once all the mourners departed, things would start to unravel ever further around him. Would his grandfather allow him to return to Eton? What about his mother? Would she have it in her to fight him? Somehow, he doubted everything and yet prayed for anything resembling his life before his father's death.

"Lord Harrington," a man said as he rested his hand on Jonas's shoulder. How could *he* be the earl now? That was his father's name, and he doubted he'd ever become accustomed to it. "It's time to head back."

He glanced up at the man as the rain continued to drip down his face. His hair was black, but had already started to turn to gray along the sides. Jonas barely knew him, but Lord Coventry had been a friend of his father's. "I'm not ready," he told him.

"George was a good man," Lord Coventry said. "He loved you."

"I know," Jonas replied woodenly. He'd long ago stopped feeling and now went through the motions. What else could he do? Lord Coventry was correct—it was long past time to go, yet he couldn't move. Once he left, it would all become too real for him. His grandfather would start barking orders, and he had years before he could be free of him. Three long years to be exact—once he turned eighteen he could seize control of his inheritance. As long as his grandfather didn't find a way to break the will. "But that doesn't change anything."

"No," Lord Coventry agreed. "He's still gone, and nothing will ever bring him back."

If Jonas were capable of crying, he'd have done so days ago. It was probably a good thing he hadn't. Any sign of weakness would have set his grandfather off. He had to be brave, and somehow find the strength to move on sooner than he'd like.

His father deserved to be mourned, but he'd understand why Jonas couldn't openly do it. "I'm ready now." Jonas didn't look at Lord Coventry. He spun on his heels and began the long trek back to Southington Castle. He hated his grandfather's home—it was as cold as he was. There wasn't anything welcoming about it.

"Lord Harrington—"

"Don't call me that," Jonas interrupted. The sound of his father's title shot pain through his already aching heart. He didn't want to think or feel. Everything reminded him of his father and the loss that he couldn't escape. The title… That was more than he could bear.

Lord Coventry cleared his throat. "It's who you are now."

"That may be." Jonas swallowed hard. "But filling my father's shoes is something I'm not yet prepared for. I can't hear his title without thinking of him and what I've lost."

"I understand," Coventry said and sighed. "You're too young to have lost your father already. If I had a son…" He shook his head. "That doesn't matter. You have a long road ahead of you, and there's probably no one you feel you can trust. You might not know it yet, but you can trust me." He paused for a moment before continuing, "What would you like me to call you?"

"Nothing," Jonas said. "I doubt we will see each other again after today."

The older man laughed. It was a foreign sound, considering their surroundings. Sadness permeated everything around them, yet the earl had found something humorous. Coventry seemed like a likeable sort and in another time, Jonas may have liked him. Somehow, he doubted he'd find anything appealing or even joyous for a long time.

Coventry gestured toward the castle in the distance. "We shall see. Come, let's get out of this rain."

The earl followed behind Jonas as they entered the castle. He didn't stay long after that. He'd spoken to the duke quietly before his departure, and the duke didn't argue or order the earl around. That alone made Jonas wonder what they'd discussed.

"Now that everyone is gone we have some things to discuss, boy." His grandfather stormed across the room and glared down at him. "Starting with your education… I was going to keep you here, but Coventry made a good point. You'll need to make connections, and those are rooted in school. So, I'll allow you to return to Eton—at least for the rest of this school year. We'll revisit that idea before the next term."

He owed the earl far more than he realized. Never had he truly believed his grandfather would allow him to return to school. "Thank you."

"Don't thank me yet," his grandfather said gruffly. "We have a lot of work ahead of us to prepare you for the dukedom."

He was barely an earl, and now he had to worry about grandfather's title? Jonas wanted to curl up into a ball and sleep for days—no, weeks. That was the cowardly way though, and he refused to give in to it. "Where is Mother?"

"She's gone to live with her sister," he replied. "Your mother is too delicate for Southington. Don't worry. Your father made sure she'd be provided for."

His mother had abandoned him? He'd always been closer to his father, but still… She left him alone with the duke, and she was well aware of his brutish nature. He had no problems using his fists to make a point. The Harrington title was prestigious, but he wouldn't have control of the estate for many years. They had plenty of funds as long as they did what the duke wanted. His father had decided to cut as many ties as possible with Southington. They lived in a small townhouse in London, and his father had invested in a profitable shipping company with the income he had available. They didn't live in splendor, but they'd been comfortable.

None of it had made the duke happy, but then nothing could. He liked having control over his family, and losing it had made him cut them out of his life. That was until his father died and he saw a way to wiggle his way back in. Now, Jonas was his ward until he gained full access to his inheritance. It was not a huge sum, but it would be enough for him to break free.

"May I be excused?" The duke hit Jonas's mouth with his fist before he was fully prepared for its impact. Jonas jerked backward involuntarily, but then gained control as quick as possible. He lifted his gaze and stared the duke in the eye, repeating his request, "May I be excused now?" Leaving without permission would prolong the torture, and he didn't want another punch to the face, or anywhere else.

The duke nodded, and Jonas left as fast as his feet would carry him. He didn't run as he wanted to because he would not give in to the duke's bullying. If he darted out of the room, his grandfather would find a reason to make him stay. Instead, he walked briskly and steadily until he reached his chambers. Only then, once the door was closed and he had privacy, did he give in to the emotions raging through him. The tears he'd held in finally flowed freely, and he grieved for his father.

London, 1812

Jonas picked up the glass of brandy on the table and took a drink. He set it back down and stared at the cards in his hand. So far, luck hadn't been on his side, and he was steadily losing what funds he had. He should have given up a long time ago but stupidly thought he'd win if he kept playing. Freedom had led him astray when it should have brought him happiness. He learned fast that the latter was an elusive emotion not meant for him.

"I think it's time to call it a night," announced Jason Thompson, Earl of Asthey. He ran his fingers through his dark blond hair and grinned like a cat that'd caught the prize mouse. "It's been a productive night."

At least it was going well for one of them. "I'm ready too." He threw his cards on the table. "I've lost too much as it is." And he had very little he could afford to lose. His grandfather still held onto most of the purse strings. Somehow, the duke had found a way to gain control over a large part of his inheritance. Jonas had won his independence a year ago, but he wasn't truly free. The one thing he had left that the duke couldn't touch was a tiny sum his maternal grandmother had left him. It barely gave him enough to live on. He needed to figure out how to raise his income, but he was at a loss on how.

"That's a shame," Asthey said. "Winning big would solve a lot of your woes."

Jonas rolled his eyes. "I need more than I'd win in a few hands of cards to solve all that." It might help if his grandfather decided to roll over and die, but no, that wouldn't happen. The old man was too bullheaded to do anything as congenial as save the world from his type of meanness. "Where is Shelby?" Gregory Cain, the Earl of Shelby, was the other member of their trio. Jonas scanned the room for Shelby's midnight locks. They were his trademark. No one else had hair quite as sinfully dark as his. His friend was nowhere to be seen in the gaming hell.

"He found a light-skirt to his liking and appropriated a room for a bit of sport."

Of course he did... Shelby was quite the rake, and relished in ravishing any willing female in his vicinity. "Should we wait?"

"He knows his way home," Asthey replied. "I rather not wait on him to finish. He might take all night, or he could come out in an hour. It's hard to say with him."

"You're right," Jonas agreed. He stood and pulled on his jacket and buttoned it over his waistcoat. "I'm tired and would rather sleep in my own bed."

They both headed to the front door and exited the gaming hell. It was still quite dark, and for once it was a rather clear night in London. The rain had been dreadful for days. The streets were filled with puddles and mud. They walked in silence for a few moments as they headed for a nearby hackney. As they stepped onto the road to cross over to the carriage, Jonas was yanked backward. He fell to the ground, his head smacking against the hard surface.

"Bloody hell," he said with a groan. "Why'd you do that?"

"I have a message for you." A big, burly man loomed over Jonas.

Jonas lifted a brow. "You might want to work on your delivery. I won't be recommending your service to anyone."

"Don't need it," the burly man replied. Jonas couldn't make out his features in the dark, but felt the sting of a fist hitting his jaw. "The message isn't the verbal kind."

Jonas was poised to throw another punch, but was jerked backward before he could land it. The man hit the ground in much the same manner as Jonas had. Served the bastard right… Jonas leapt to his feet before the other man could get up. He rubbed his hand over his sore jaw. "Took you long enough." He turned to whom he'd thought was Asthey, but was shocked to find Lord Coventry instead.

"Where's Asthey?"

"There." Coventry pointed in the distance. He was battling a ruffian of his own. He landed a solid blow, and the man fell to the ground. "What is going on?"

"Unfortunately, this is the work of your grandfather," he replied. A hint of sadness echoed through his voice. "I heard a rumor and came to investigate the veracity of it."

"And?" Jonas didn't like where this conversation was going. His grandfather could do a lot of damage if he wanted to, and it appeared as if he'd decided to employ his power. He had to have all the information Coventry possessed so he could form a plan of his own. His grandfather's contacts were extensive and his reach even farther. In order to beat him at his own game Jonas might have to fight dirty.

"I'm afraid it was correct by the looks of things," Coventry answered.

Asthey joined them, shaking his hand in the air as he walked. "That hurts more than I want to admit. I might need to learn a thing or two about throwing a proper punch."

Coventry nodded. "I might be able to help you both." He turned to Asthey. "Go inside and fetch your friend, Shelby. I have a proposition for you all."

Asthey didn't question Coventry's order. He nodded and headed back into the gaming hell. Jonas watched him until he disappeared inside, and then turned back to Coventry. "What do you know?"

"Far more than you do," he replied cryptically. "The duke has plans for you, and he's not happy with your reluctance to follow them."

"That's something I know far too well." He wished the old man would leave him alone already. "Was this his way of forcing me to go to Southington?"

"I'm not entirely sure what he hoped to accomplish tonight," Coventry admitted. "I know he arranged it, and I'm here to help if you'll allow it."

Jonas was so tired of constantly fighting with his grandfather. There had to be a way to stop him from coming after him again and again. "What do you have in mind?"

Asthey and Shelby came out of the gaming hell and joined them. Shelby carried his cravat in his hand and was straightening his jacket. "This better be important," Shelby muttered. "The chit was…"

"We don't need to know," Asthey said, interrupting him.

Coventry smiled. "I believe you boys will fit right in."

"I don't follow," Jonas said, then frowned. "Fit in where?"

"A very special club," he replied. "Come along.

I'll explain everything and how it'll help you with Southington, your social life, and even financially, if you like."

He didn't understand how a club could do all that, but he was willing to hear Coventry out. He had saved him from being beaten, and as long as Jonas had his two friends with him, he didn't see the harm. They could decide together if it was something worth doing. They'd stuck together this long.

They followed Coventry to a nearby carriage and climbed inside. It rolled across the cobbled street with ease. The interior was plush, and the seats rather comfortable. Jonas had never ridden in a carriage so fine. After a short drive, the carriage stopped. They all got outside to find an elegant townhouse with a W emblazoned near the door. Where were they? What had Coventry said earlier? Something about a club.

"Where are we?" Asthey asked vocalizing Jonas's thoughts.

"Doesn't look like much," Shelby replied. "Why'd I leave that lovely lass again?

Coventry pulled a key out of his pocket that had the same W on the top of it. He pushed it into the lock and opened the door." "Gentleman, please come inside." He led them from the foyer into the main part of the house.

The outside expertly disguised the decadence found inside. Rich velvet draped the windows. The settees, chaise lounge, and every chair in the place had similar color scheme of dark red and burnished brown. To the side was a long cherry banister that wound around an elaborate staircase. To the side was a large room with a blazing fireplace. Several men sat at one of the tables as they played cards. Each one had a beautiful, scantily clad woman on their lap. Jonas's mouth fell open at everything he saw, and he couldn't believe he didn't know the place existed. He turned to Coventry and said, "You have our attention. Want to explain this to us now?" He continued to stare at the luxuriousness of his surroundings.

Coventry smiled. "Welcome to the club. You have been nominated for admission—if you want to join. There are rules, of course," Coventry told them. "Nothing too extreme, but you should all find them reasonable. Keep the club a secret, and you forfeit your membership once you marry—only the leader of the group is allowed to have a wife and retain his membership. If you're wondering who that is—I am the currently in charge of the club and its members." He glanced at each one of them and asked, "Do you wish to be a part of all this?" He held his arms out wide.

They all nodded immediately. Jonas didn't give it much thought, and figured the other two hadn't either. The sheer excess of the place had won them over. The rest he could figure out later.

It was a decision he never regretted…

CHAPTER 1

London, 1823

Dark gray clouds floated in the sky above, threatening to unleash rain upon everyone who dared to walk the streets of London. Lady Marian Lindsay stared up at them as she chewed her bottom lip. It was not a good sign, and she hoped the bad omen didn't lead to a disastrous meeting with Sir Anthony Davis. Not that rain wasn't commonplace in England—because it most certainly graced the country with regularity; however, Marian's luck never held when it deigned to fall from the sky. So her meeting with Sir Anthony would surely be doomed.

Nonetheless, she fully intended to go through

with it. She had plans, and Sir Anthony stood in the way of them. Without his permission, she'd never become a part of the Royal Medical Society. They had this misbegotten notion medicine and women didn't mix. She hoped to change his mind and have him recommend her for admission.

She'd been studying medicine and herbs her entire life. All right, maybe not that long, but it felt like it. Her interest started almost a decade ago after her aunt and uncle's death. They'd both been in a terrible carriage accident near her family estate. Her father was the Earl of Coventry. Her uncle, the Earl of Frossly, married her Aunt Belinda and became a part of the family. After their death, Marian's mother had been desperate with grief and the loss of her beloved younger sister.

Everything in Marian's life changed after that. Her two cousins came to live with them, and her mother became sick following their arrival—leaving her launch into society, as well as her cousin's, forgotten. Not that she had minded especially once her mother succumbed to her illness and they lost her forever. Her grief had been too great, and she'd decided she wanted more in life. Marian didn't want to marry and have children. She had much loftier goals—like becoming an actual physician and making a living helping people.

Which brought her back to Sir Anthony—he had to let her into the society. This was the next step to gaining the knowledge she needed to become a doctor. She glanced up at the sky once more.

"Please hold off until I'm done," she begged. "I need a little bit of time." She quickened her pace until she reached Sir Anthony's building and pushed the door open. Marian entered as the rain started to fall. It pounded against the street, creating puddles almost instantly. She shut the door and blew out a relieved breath.

Someone cleared their throat. She turned and found two men standing inside, staring at her with a modicum of surprise etched on their faces. The older gentleman must have been Sir Anthony. He had dark hair streaked with gray. The other gentleman was rather handsome—dashing even. He had dark hair and devilish blue eyes. Much to her chagrin, she'd always found him enticing, and not because he was the most gorgeous male she'd ever seen. There was something about him that made the heart inside her chest beat heavily. Marian's whole body hummed with some unnamable energy. Jonas Parker, the esteemable Earl of Harrington, would always put her at a disadvantage, and sometimes she believed he knew it too. *Damn him.* "Hello, my lord," Marian greeted him and then turned to the older man. "Sir Anthony." She hoped her presumption was correct and he was the man she thought, or wouldn't that be embarrassing...

"Lady Marian," Lord Harrington said in a slow drawl. "Does your father know you're in this part of town?"

Drat. Of course that would be the first thing he'd ask—at least he hadn't corrected her about Sir Anthony. "My father is well aware of my activities." That wasn't entirely a lie. He did know she hoped to be a doctor and humored her. He didn't really believe she'd succeed, but she planned on proving him wrong. Men had all the advantages in society and women were given little say in their lives. Something she hated to the depths of her soul. "You needn't worry about me."

"What may we assist you with?" Sir Anthony asked. "Did the rain drive you inside?"

Lord Harrington lifted a brow. "I don't think that's it at all." He kept his gaze on Marian, unnerving her. He saw too much, and she rather disliked the scrutiny. "You're here because of your little project, aren't you?"

Anyone acquainted with her father, and therefore her, was aware of her desire to be a doctor. Her father boasted of her hobby even though he doubted her. It was his way of giving her his support. Not that it was a lot or even a stamp of approval, but it had managed to aid her in her quest thus far. "What if I am?" She jutted out her chin. "You aim to prevent me from taking the next step?"

He held out his hands in front of him. "Far be it from me to step in front of a bluestocking on a mission. By all means, say your piece and see if Sir Anthony is willing to assist you."

Sir Anthony glanced back and forth between them, but Marian barely noticed. She was irritated more than she should be. Lord Harrington was being nice by allowing her to speak—a sardonic, arrogant, and presumptuous...*man*. Rolling her eyes would not help her convince Sir Anthony she should be a part of the Royal Medical Society. She took a deep breath to calm herself. Calling him names inside her head would not further her goals. She had to pull herself together and try to present herself in the best light to Sir Anthony.

"You require something from me?" Anthony asked as he gave her his full attention. "What is it?"

"Well," she started. This was much harder than she thought it would be. "I have a request I hope you'll agree to."

"Oh?"

That was it. Nothing else from him or any encouragement for her to go on. Lord Harrington, the rogue, leaned against a nearby table and crossed his arms over his chest. He had a wicked grin on his too handsome face. If Marian wasn't a lady, she'd do something to wipe that knowing smile away. Someone should put him in his place, and maybe then he wouldn't be so condescending.

"I've been studying for a while to be a physician…"

"You have?" Sir Anthony scrunched his eyebrows together. "Your father knows you're doing this?"

"Well, yes," she said. "I did mention he was aware of my activities…"

"She's a bluestocking," Lord Harrington added. "You know how they are when they get an idea in their head. It's why I didn't stop her when she came in, if you'll recall."

Marian gave in and rolled her eyes. She couldn't

help herself any longer. Why did she have to be attracted to him? He drove her mad in more ways than she could count, yet he was the one man her body became alive near. She hated him for it.

"Thank you, my lord." She pasted a cheerful smile on her face. "You give glowing recommendations."

"It's the least I can do," he replied with that sinful voice of his. It sent shivers down her spine. "As you can see, Sir Anthony is quite scandalized with your chosen hobby. He's gone mute with the shock of it."

Damn him, he was right. Sir Anthony stared at her as if she were a bug to be studied in length. He hadn't said a word in several heartbeats. "I had hoped you'd foster my admission into the Royal—"

"Absolutely not," he responded with vehemence. "Ladies do not become doctors or study anything. I don't understand this generation and their need to poke their noses in things they best not be a part of."

"Some ladies find science and knowledge enticing," Marian said as she lifted her head in defiance. "Intelligence is quite an attractive asset to inspire to."

"Touché," Lord Harrington agreed. "But I'd take it a step further and suggest there are things a gentleman finds more attractive in a lady than what's inside their head."

She shook her head. "I didn't come here to debate the qualities one looks for in a potential spouse. I want to become an active member of the Royal Medical Society."

"That's not going to happen, my dear. I'm afraid women are not allowed and never will be." Sir Anthony squared his shoulders, preparing for battle. Good, she planned on giving him something to fight about.

"Never is a long time to adhere to," Lady Marian replied. "Do you want to limit yourself when there are infinite possibilities if you'd open yourself up to them?"

"It's not up to me," Sir Anthony told her. "Society has rules for a reason. Go home and do something more ladylike. It truly is for the best."

She narrowed her gaze and pursed her lips together. *Ladylike*? He was much worse than Lord Harrington. At least the earl pretended to give her the space to argue her stance. Sir Anthony was an old-fashioned sycophant. He thought playing up to her feminine tributes would make her abandon her calling and do a bit of embroidery instead. Why could a man do anything he wanted, but a woman had inadequate options? If she decided to take up water colors or the pianoforte, they'd encourage her. Being a doctor though? That was a ridiculous notion.

"Thank you for your sage advice," Marian replied with false sweetness. "I'll leave you gentleman to whatever you were discussing. It's time for me to return home. Good day." She curtsied and turned to the door.

"Wait," Lord Harrington demanded as he stepped forward. "I'll escort you."

"There's no need," she explained. Marian did not want him following her home. If he spoke to her father, then much more than a failed attempt to gain entry into the Royal Medical Society would befall her. "I managed to arrive here safely without an escort. I don't need one to see I find my way home."

"Perhaps," he replied cordially. "But I will be by your side every step of the way regardless. I'd never forgive myself if something happened to you and I could have prevented it." The corner of his mouth lifted enticingly. "I admire your father, and for that alone I'd see you safely to the ends of the Earth. Nothing you can say will talk me out of this."

Damn him. She cursed him for the thousandth

time in the space of a half hour. At that rate, she'd start saying it aloud. There was no way she'd win in an argument with him. The easiest way would be to agree, but that irritated her nonetheless.

"Fine," she replied. "Have it your way."

"I always do," he retorted. "Good of you to see that." His blue eyes practically twinkled with mischief. He was a conceited scoundrel.

She ground her teeth together and refrained from responding. Instead, she spun on her heels and exited the building and Sir Anthony's misogyny. She would not give up on her dream. There had to be another way, and if there was, she'd find it.

The rain hadn't stopped while she was inside the shop. It beat against her in a rapid staccato, making her wish she'd stayed inside a bit longer, or procured a carriage. Why hadn't she planned this a little better? Because that would have made sense... She'd been blinded by her ambition and the need to be a part of something much bigger than herself. One day she'd learn the benefit of a well laid plan. Unfortunately, that day was not this one.

"Come with me," Lord Harrington leaned down and spoke directly into her ear. His heat enveloped her, making her forget where she was for a moment. He picked up her hand and rested it on his arm to lead her in the direction of his choosing. "My carriage is around the corner."

She blinked several times as rain continued to drown out the sound of the London Street. What was happening to her? She shook her head and did as Lord Harrington said. A carriage in this kind of weather was desirable, and for the first time since she saw him inside Sir Anthony's place, she was happy to have him near.

Thankfully, Lord Harrington's carriage wasn't far away. He helped her inside, but unfortunately, she was already soaked through. She couldn't wait to return home and put some distance between them. Uncomfortable wasn't a strong enough word to describe how he made her feel, and it didn't help that she was drenched from head to toe. She had to look a fright… What nonsense.

Why did she care if she looked less than desirable? Lord Harrington wasn't a potential suitor even if she was looking for a husband. He was one of the biggest rogues of the ton, and she was firmly on the shelf. Marian was a bluestocking and a spinster in the making, as untouchable as possible and quite content with that fate. Her pent up wantonness could dwindle down to nothing. She didn't need a man to find happiness.

Maybe she'd found a spot of luck in a sea of bad fortune. So, she'd taken a couple steps backward from her main goal. That didn't mean she couldn't find a way to move forward. For now, she'd allow Lord Harrington to see her home, and then she'd meet with her two closest friends to make a new plan. This was not the end of anything. Marian chose to see to it as a beginning. The likes of Sir Anthony and Lord Harrington would not discourage her.

EXCERPT: CONFESSIONS OF A HELLION

BLUESTOCKINGS DEFYING ROGUES BOOK SEVEN

DAWN BROWER

USA TODAY
BESTSELLING AUTHOR

Dawn Brower

Confessions of a Hellion

PROLOGUE

Weston Manor, 1823

They entered the ballroom. It was already filled to capacity. Even if they remained wallflowers, they'd be unable to avoid all the guests. Everyone must have accepted the invite. The Duke and Duchess of Weston didn't entertain often, and they were all probably curious. Lady Samantha couldn't blame them. She had been rather intrigued herself. She loved balls and dancing. Being invited to one of the exclusive country events at the end of the season thrilled her. She scanned the room for the duchess and found her on the far edge of the dance floor.

Marian only cared about one thing. Securing

the Duchess of Weston's assistance in learning to be a doctor. She glanced around the room until she located her, then turned to Samantha and Kaitlin. "If you'll excuse me," she said to them. "I'm going to talk to the duchess."

"Don't forget to ask her this time," Samantha said. "I see Lord Darcy; I'm heading in his direction." She didn't really want the Earl of Darcy's attention, but it sounded good to say she wanted to dance with him. "I'd hate for him to not be able to locate me. Come with me, Katie, so I'm not standing alone."

"So you can leave me stranded as you run off with him?" Kaitlin grumbled under her breath. "You'll owe me for this."

"Don't worry, dear," Samantha replied as she dragged Kaitlin with her. "I'll find you a dance partner too. Isn't that Lord Asthey talking to Lord Darcy?" Her heart thundered in her chest. While she hadn't really wanted to see Lord Darcy, she did want to see Lord Asthey. He was so handsome. Both Lord Darcy and Lord Asthey were blond, had gorgeous blue eyes, and amazing physiques. Judging them by looks alone wasn't enough though. Only one of them made her heart race and filled her with excitement. The problem of course was he didn't notice her as anything more than his friend's little sister.

Kaitlin sighed and let Samantha lead her to the two earls. "I don't need to dance." She shook her head vigorously. "I can find a book to read and sit in the corner."

Samantha stopped and stared at her friend. "You will do no such thing." How could Kaitlin not want to dance? "Do you not like Lord Asthey?" That seemed even worse somehow. Samantha adored him. She wanted him for herself, but gave up on that notion a while ago. If she couldn't get pleasure from dancing with him perhaps her friend could. Not that she wanted Lord Asthey to fall in love with Kaitlin, but he seemed to like her. Samantha wasn't so selfish as to not wish her friend happiness. Even if it felt as if she were being stabbed in the heart every time Lord Asthey smiled fondly at Kaitlin... She shook that pain away and pasted a smile on her face.

"Lord Asthey is likeable enough," Kaitlin said in a good-natured tone. "But I don't like dancing." She wrinkled her nose in disgust.

"Nonsense," Samantha said and waved her hand. "You just haven't found the right partner yet."

She narrowed her gaze. Was that her brother lounging in the corner? Samantha blew out a breath. She'd have to be careful. If Gregory, Lord Shelby, her overprotective brother thought she was getting too attached to the Earl of Darcy he might act rashly. In her brother's mind no one was good enough for her. Especially one of the wicked earls, as they dubbed themselves. Unfortunately, Lord Asthey was also in that particular group. Shelby adored his friends. He just didn't want any of his friends to pay any attention to his little sister.

Kaitlin placed her hand on Samantha's arm. "I really do not wish to dance."

What was she supposed to do? Kaitlin would be more comfortable hiding in a corner. She had to help her friend break out of her shell in some way. If she insisted on gluing herself to a wall she'd never find love. Kaitlin deserved to find someone that would adore her. Samantha wanted to help guide her there. If she couldn't have the one man she loved, then at least Kaitlin would. "One dance," Samantha said. "After that we can leave the ballroom if you wish."

Kaitlin's shoulders drooped. She closed her eyes and took a deep breath. "Fine," she said. "I'll dance one but after that I don't want you to pressure me into anything else I don't wish to do. I'll have your word on it." She glared at Samantha.

"I promise," Samantha said earnestly and crossed her finger over her heart. "You may rely upon it."

She looped her arm through Kaitlin's and led her the rest of the way to Lord Darcy and Lord Asthey. They were deep in conversation when they arrived next to them.

"I guess we are co-captains at this year's cricket match," Darcy said. "We have more options for teammates here. What should we ask for as our prize when we win?"

"A little arrogant of you to count our winnings before they're earned, isn't it?" Asthey lifted a brow. "Shelby is damn good at the game. I should know."

They both stopped talking when they arrived. "We're not interrupting are we?" Samantha batted her eyelashes at them. She was well aware of their yearly cricket match. Whenever she could she'd sneak out to watch some of their private matches. Not all of them took place at country parties. One thing stayed true throughout the years. They all played and the four of them divided up differently each year. That was how they kept things between them fair.

Kaitlin had a far away expression on her face. Her friend was probably daydreaming about something she wouldn't share. Samantha doubted she had heard anything the two earls had been discussing. Sometimes Kaitlin lived in a world of her own. Samantha wished she could lose herself in her own mind every now and then. She had too many plans to live in a make-believe world. Samantha glanced at her friend then at the two earls. "Are you going to dance this evening?" Perhaps a little blunt but Samantha wasn't known for her shy and demure demeanor. Her brother often called her a hellion. She wouldn't apologize for who she was for any reason.

"I…" Asthey stumbled over the words.

"Why of course," Darcy said smoothly. He bowed. "Would you care to dace Lady Samantha?"

Why couldn't Asthey have asked her to dance? He had started to speak first. Would he have actually asked if Darcy hadn't interrupted him? Somehow she doubted it. "That would be lovely," she answered him. She managed to keep a bright smile on her face even though she didn't feel anything resembling excitement. She held out her hand to him and he led her to the floor. At least it wasn't a waltz. She didn't want to dance such an intimate set with Lord Darcy.

Asthey bowed to Kaitlin and said something to her. She shook her head vigorously. Did her friend just decline to dance with him? Samantha seethed inwardly. Kaitlin had the one thing Samantha coveted before her and she had said no. That was… wrong. She turned to Darcy as he led her through the dance. They didn't talk much and for that she was thankful. Asthey and Kaitlin strolled around the room. Samantha was green with jealousy but she tamped it down.

"Are you enjoying the ball?" Lord Darcy asked.

"Of course," she answered smoothly. "Are you?"

"Yes," he said. "It's been quite entertaining."

This had to be the most mundane conversation she'd ever had. Through it all she kept the smile on her face. She also kept track of every step Lord Asthey and Kaitlin took. They seemed to be having an animated conversation. Whatever Lord Asthey was saying Kaitlin found riveting. She wished she could hear it. Hell, Samantha just wished she could hold Lord Asthey's attention as long as Kaitlin seemed to be holding it.

Would he court her? Dance with her? Love her?

Would Samantha wake one day to find an engagement announcement in the Times? Her heart broke at the thought. How was she to survive in a world where one of her best friends married the man she loved? What was wrong with her? She had to let him go. He clearly didn't see her the same way. She turned her attention to Darcy. He at least looked at her as an attractive female. He might not love her, but he appreciated her.

The dance came to an end and Lord Darcy led her to the edge of the dance floor. He bowed and said, "Thank you for the dance."

"It was my pleasure, Lord Darcy." Where were Kaitlin and Asthey? She had lost track of them at the end of the dance.

"If you'll excuse me I see Lord Harrington. There is something I must discuss with him."

Samantha wasn't a fool. He would want to discuss their upcoming cricket match. She might try to eavesdrop later. Samantha didn't want to miss the pertinent details. She wanted to be able to watch and secretly cheer for Lord Asthey, but she could gather that information later. It was far more important to locate Kaitlin and Lord Asthey. She curtsied. "Until next time."

His lips twitched. "I look forward to it." With

those words he left her alone and headed toward Lord Harrington.

At that moment she caught a glimpse of Kaitlin out of the corner of her eye. She was alone. Where had Asthey gone? Samantha scanned the room feverishly. He'd disappeared. She lost her chance at securing a dance with him. The strands of a waltz filled the room. She turned to leave the ballroom before anyone noticed the crestfallen expression on her face. She ran right into a male. He had a hard muscular chest that most women might find appealing. Samantha glanced up and met Lord Asthey's gaze.

"My apologies," he said. "I should have been paying attention better." He glanced past her to the other side of the room. He'd been heading toward Harrington too. She'd let him go plan with his friends but this was the only chance she had with him. Samantha wanted one dance. Just one. Was that too much to ask?

"You can make it up to me by dancing with me." She smiled softly, silently begging him. "Please." It was the waltz. She wanted to feel his arms around her. So she could pretend for a few brief moments he loved her.

"I..." He swallowed hard. "Of course." Lord

Asthey held out his hand to her and led her to the floor.

Samantha felt as if she were floating on clouds. Lord Asthey was a marvelous dancer and led her expertly around the floor. This was a dream. One she had every night but until now hadn't experienced in reality. Of course it wasn't exactly as she had dreamed it. In her fantasies he confessed his love and asked her to marry him. A lady couldn't have everything could she?

She would remember this dance for the rest of her life. It probably would be the only dance she had with him. If this were all she would have she'd cherish it. When she was old and alone she could look back on it with fondness. If she were brave enough she'd confess her feelings. Even hellions had trouble spilling all their secrets though. Some confessions wouldn't unburden the soul. It was best she kept her deepest desires to herself. She wouldn't want to scare Lord Asthey away. It would break her heart even more if she never saw him again.

The dance came to an end and he led her off the floor. They hadn't said a word throughout the entire dance. That was all right with her. It was enough to have had this one dance. She smiled at him hoping he could see how much she cared. He didn't. He bowed and made his excuses. It was over before it ever had a chance to begin. Lord Asthey left her alone and went toward his friends. Samantha's smile wobbled a little. She had to leave before the world became privy to her anguish. Without saying a word she turned on her heels and exited the ballroom. Kaitlin could take care of herself. Marian was still there after all… Samantha barely contained her tears until she reached her chambers. Once there she let go and cried all her pain out.

When she had no more tears to shed she sat up and wiped her face. There. That was done. Now she could move on and find a man who would love her. Lord Asthey didn't know what he was missing.

If only she could make herself believe that…

Manufactured by Amazon.ca
Bolton, ON